PENGUIN BOOKS

Quintessence

Portrait by Marianne Muggeridge — Oeo, Taranaki
Photo by Richard Wotten

Christine Leov Lealand's natural curiosity about
human nature combined with five years as a
sexological counsellor has given her a thousand
experiences and images of us in the bedroom
(and lots of other places). Born in the South
Island she now lives in the North Island with
her partner.

Quintessence

Erotic Adventures of Fantasy & Desire

CHRISTINE LEOV LEALAND

PENGUIN BOOKS

PENGUIN BOOKS

Penguin Books (NZ) Ltd, cnr Airborne and Rosedale Roads, Albany,
Auckland 1310, New Zealand
Penguin Books Ltd, 27 Wrights Lane, London W8 5TZ, England
Penguin Putnam Inc, 375 Hudson Street, New York, NY 10014,
United States
Penguin Books Australia Ltd, 487 Maroondah Highway,
Ringwood, Australia 3134
Penguin Books Canada Ltd, 10 Alcorn Avenue, Toronto,
Ontario, Canada M4V 3B2
Penguin Books (South Africa) Pty Ltd, 5 Watkins Street,
Denver Ext 4, 2094, South Africa
Penguin Books India (P) Ltd, 11, Community Centre, Panchsheel Park,
New Delhi 110 017, India

Penguin Books Ltd, Registered Offices: Harmondsworth, Middlesex, England

First published by Penguin Books (NZ) Ltd, 1999
5 7 9 10 8 6
Copyright © Christine Leov Lealand 1999

Illustrations by Sandy Collins
Designed by Mary Egan and Mike Wagg
Typeset by Egan-Reid Ltd, Auckland
Printed in Australia by Australian Print Group, Maryborough

Dedicated to everyone who knows that sex is better than drugs

And

To all who encouraged me as I wrote.

If you think you feature in this book please introduce yourself.
I'm always interested in meeting figments of my imagination.

What holds the world together, as I have learned from bitter experience, is sexual intercourse.

But *fuck* the real thing, *cunt*, the real thing, seems to contain some unidentified element, which is far more dangerous than nitroglycerine.

Henry Miller

Tropic of Capricorn, 1939

I

*T*iffany walked up the stairs and admired the sign over the door of her advertising agency. 'Tiffany & Co', it said. They'd put a lot of thought into their image and the sign was bold but elegant at the same time. The door was closed. Through the antique glass Tiffany thought she could see that the office was empty. She glanced around the semicircle of computer-laden desks as she quietly pushed open the door. No, not all the girls were out visiting clients. Louise was in front of her computer, staring at the screen.

She's sitting in an odd way, thought Tiffany, walking

quietly over to her. The crepe soles of her ankle-length boots made no sound on the polished floor as Tiffany snuck up to get a glimpse of the latest creative masterpiece from Louise's wild brain.

Louise had a leg thrown over the arm of her office chair and she seemed to be trembling . . . Tiffany peeked at the screen. Displayed were two women. One was naked, harnessed and collared with studded leather, kneeling on all fours. Standing over her was a strong stern-looking woman wearing riding jodhpurs, jacket open showing her breasts and, it seemed, just about to beat the kneeling woman with her riding crop.

Louise had her right hand vibrating between her legs, lifting up her panties, and her left was moving inside her white silky blouse. Tiffany smiled, leaned down beside Louise and said softly in her ear, 'Which customer are you going to sell this to, Lou?' Louise gasped and hurriedly covered herself, sat up and tucked her blouse in.

'Sorry, Tiff — I . . .' she paused, blushing, 'I haven't got an explanation . . .' She leaned forward and minimised the window on the screen.

Tiffany frowned. 'You realise I could have been a client?' she asked sternly, hands on hips, staring down at dishevelled but glowing Louise.

Louise looked up at her, flushed and trembling. 'I'm

8

awfully sorry, really I am – I'm just *so* horny! You know! You know how it is! I haven't found anyone since Bill and I split. And that was nearly two years ago.' She turned and glared at the Bart Simpson desktop on the computer screen. 'I'm too young to quit on sex!' she said angrily, 'I'm only 30!' She fell forward in despair onto her keyboard. The computer began beeping and clanging; her long straight dark hair fell in a slow cascade over her arms. She began sobbing in long slow wrenching cries. Tiffany looked at the nape of Louise's neck and unconsciously licked her lips.

'By the time I've done here for the day and picked up Sampson from daycare, given him the attention he needs and made dinner each night, I'm too tired for anything – and then I always feel horny in the afternoons. It's hard to ignore.' Louise's voice was muffled but sounded angry and desperate.

'Today you couldn't ignore it?' Tiffany asked, massaging her friend's shoulders.

'Yes.' Louise was still trembling. Tiffany leaned forward and clicked the mouse to bring back the telltale photo. Then she clicked the link to the next photo in the series.

The nude slave girl was now being ridden like a horse by the woman with the whip. She sat there proudly, holding the reins tightly. The bit cut deeply into the girl's red painted mouth. From the rear of the girl there protruded a swishy, perky tail.

'This is what turns you on?' asked Tiffany, surprised. Then she queried more softly, 'Do you want to be pony or rider?' Tiffany hoped she sounded calm but inside she was wildly excited. Louise looked at the screen, gasped softly, considered. Tiffany ran her fingers up the nape of Louise's neck and slowly twined that long dark hair tightly around her hand.

'Oh!' whispered Louise 'I'd love to be the girl who is forced to be the horse!' She shut her eyes, shuddered and took a deep breath. 'I've never told anyone that,' she whispered.

Tiffany pulled Louise's head back, arching her spine against the chair back. 'And I'd love to be that lady rider,' she stated. Her voice calm and firm. 'With you as my little pony.' She leaned down and blew softly into Louise's ear. Louise burst into tears again.

'Don't tease me! It's all just a fantasy, no more than a fantasy!' she wailed. Tiffany held her tight and stood back, considering what to say next, looking down longingly at Louise's aroused body.

'I suppose fantasies are not for living out, are they, Louise?' She pulled harder on Louise's hair, hurting her just a little, arching her body more. 'Just for wanking over, are they?'

'Yes, yes, that's all! Just for thinking about. That's all!'

cried Louise, her face streaked with tears and stretched by the tight grip Tiffany had on her hair.

'I don't agree with you, Lou. I certainly don't agree with you. I have lived out lots of my fantasies and will do so again. Why can't you?' She released Louise who grabbed a handful of tissues, blew her nose, then hurried to the ladies' loos.

Tiffany went over to the big windows which overlooked the brightly coloured play blocks of the container port and, further out, yachts on the harbour glittering in the spring sunshine. 'Should I risk it?' she wondered aloud, trembling at the excitement, the danger.

Dare I have an affair in my own office? In front of my beloved partner, Sam? Oh shit — Sam! Sam — lesbian all her life. Sam, so moody and yet hot; critical and yet indefinably sexy. Her long lovely muscular legs, her blonde shaggy fine hair she always cropped short in a #2.

Sam had known she was a lesbian from the time she was ten years old. At first it seemed a bit strange to Tiffany, loving a woman and forgetting about men. But it was easy with Sam as her lover. Tiffany sighed, thinking of Sam's lovely breasts, just the right size and shape. Venus de Milo. No lipstick. Husky masculine voice, Levi jeans just like the butch dykes in books. Pierced ears and nipples. Zebra-striped hair this week. Not that Sam was into anything kinky, worst luck.

It sounds like a stupid idea and yet . . . I adore Lou . . .

How many years have we known each other now? Three, nearly four? She sat on the sofa, gazed into the far distance, smiled and shook her head. Ah! Look at Lou, what gets her off! How can she go hunting for that on the weekends, eh? With a little pre-schooler tagging along. The chances of her finding that sort of trade are pretty remote, even here in the central city. Even if she could afford the heavy bondage thing. But together we could get something happening. Tiffany felt the heat of lust rising in her body and she trembled at the thought of Louise, how horny she was. What a turn-on.

Would Sam really mind? Would she? In her heart Tiffany knew Sam would. She'd mind a great deal if Tiffany were anything more than friends with another woman, even if they never made love. And who could not make love with the delicious Louise?

I wonder about my relationship with Sam, though. It has lost a lot of intensity recently. Sam won't eat me out these days and that's what turns me on more than anything. It's frustrating that sex has stopped being satisfying.

God, Louise seems so strong, yet she wants to be a slave. I suppose it's part of feeling safe, secure, being a child again. I can understand that. She's had a lot of stress since she left that waste of space Bill. ·

Louise came back from the loo and walked over to stand

beside Tiffany. She looked out the window. She had fixed her make-up and appeared almost normal again, but Tiffany could feel her vibrating like a tuning fork pitched higher than the human ear could hear. She put her arm around Louise and gave her a squeeze then turned to face her and, suddenly making up her mind, said abruptly, 'Meet me tomorrow at Marie Antoinette's on the waterfront. We'll have coffee and talk, OK? What about 2 pm?' Louise nodded, appreciative of Tiffany letting her off this serious breach of office etiquette. 'Now! What about that flyer design? The final idea has to be in tomorrow!'

Tiffany went to her desk and began downloading her e-mail for the day. Louise was soon clicking away at her computer as if nothing had happened and yet stealing into her heart was a small sly hope, a stab of excitement. Louise no longer felt so desperately alone. What did Tiffany mean? Fantasies can be lived out?

Sam burst through the door and they both jumped nervously. 'Guess what?' she crowed excitedly. 'We've just landed a big one!'

Tiffany stood up. 'You mean?' she said, heart in her mouth.

'Yes! The National Art Gallery! We are just the hottest advertising agency! They want us to do all their stuff including national tours for the next two years!'

'Fantastic Sam! You did it!' Louise and Tiffany hugged her enthusiastically. Tiffany kissed her on the mouth and kept on hugging her while Louise got out the champagne. Excitedly they discussed the contract, their newest ideas, thinking of the fat fee they would get. Sam put her latest CD on the sound system. The big room was suddenly full of laughter.

The champagne was gone when Bet and Fiona walked in. Bet seemed upset, holding a plastic pack of tissues in her hand and pressing one to her nose. Her eyes were red. Fiona had her arm around Bet and guided her over to the sofa beside the window. Tiff, Lou and Sam watched them enter in silent amazement.

'Come on! Let us into the secret!' Fiona demanded, walking over to them. 'I bet you've drunk all the champers, you greedy buggers!'

'How did you guess?' asked Sam, striding over to Fiona and throwing an arm around her. 'But you are lucky. I bought us a whole case! I just got the confirmation – we've got the Art Gallery contract!'

'Fantastic!' said Fiona and waltzed with Sam over to the bottles and glasses.

'Wow!' said Bet, from the sofa, cheering visibly. 'Did you really? I said you could do it and you have!' Tiffany went over to sit beside Bet, taking her a foaming flute of champagne.

'What's wrong, sweetheart?' she asked softly. Tiffany

hated it when any of her friends, her co-workers, were out of sorts.

'I – uh . . . ' Bet hung her head. 'We were at the National Library looking up some stuff for the new postal contract when I saw someone I knew.' Tiffany waited. Bet took a few gulps of her wine. 'It was an old boyfriend, actually. I got a real shock. I sort of knew he was here but it hadn't ever sunk in. He didn't recognise me, of course. I – I didn't know I was so fond of him.' Tears flowed down her face once more.

Tiffany hugged her. 'Yeah?' She was immediately curious. She hadn't come across one of Bet's old boyfriends before. Bet had tried out all the available men she'd met since she had been in Wellington – dozens of them, and none lasted longer than an evening. She always said they weren't really interested in her, just her large breasts. She refused to go out a second time with a guy who looked at her tits or her bum all night and tried to pay for sex with an expensive dinner and flowers. The result was that her taste in men was a bit of a mystery to them all.

Never bloody rains but it pours, Tiffany thought ruefully, looking over at Louise, Fiona and Sam still excitedly discussing the new contract. She tried not to focus on Lou particularly, or Sam. She felt guilty about her feelings for both of them, then a spark of anger ignited within her. Why shouldn't I love both of them? Why not? What damn law is there against it? She hugged Bet tight.

'Tell us about it when you are ready, Bet.'

Bet sat and sipped champagne. The bubbles stung her reddened nose and she blinked rapidly as she looked out over the city. Her thoughts drifted back to that time so long ago now, when she was 19 and ready for anything . . .

2

$\mathcal{G}$od, how silly! I remember . . . he always loved Johnson's baby powder. Bet laughed to herself and looked up at the ceiling. He seduced me with baby powder, didn't he? He's a backbench MP now and all I can think about is how he used to play mummies and daddies with me. She rubbed her hand over her face, wiped her eyes. Blew her nose again.

He wears a suit now and everything — what a guy! Bet giggled to herself. I couldn't imagine him in a suit then. I met him at an Invercargill RSA do. You know, lots of drunken old soldiers milling around standing on your feet while their wives sit in the corners catching up on the gossip. I'd gone along to keep mum company. She liked the RSA so long as she had company.

So I was sitting there, bored out of my tiny mind, when this man, a guy about my age, big handsome front-row forward type, sat down beside me. I glanced at him, brown skin with thick black hair curling over his eyes – I didn't dare look at his shorts or his thighs. I stared at his huge knees instead.

'Gidday,' he said to my tits.

'Gidday yourself,' I said. I ducked down to stare up into his big blues. 'Are you going to talk to me or to my tits?' He cleared his throat and sat back, pretending to look nonchalant. His huge thighs were spread wide, his arms folded – he didn't know where to put himself, actually. He blushed – really red.

'Did ya see the footy today?' he tried again.

'No, should I have?'

'Yeah. I scored two tries,' he said in an arrogant sort of shy way.

'Great – good on ya,' I said, looking him over. 'Not even a scratch – you must be lucky.'

'Yeah, I am, but I'm the biggest player on both teams,' he admitted, looking down at his huge hands. 'Er – would ya be interested in going out for a coffee?' He looked me in the eye this time.

I thought about it. 'OK,' I said, 'what about now?' The RSA had weakened me with boredom. I said ta-ta to mum and we dodged our way outside. The main street was very quiet as we wandered along looking for a tearooms that might still be open. In the end we found a grotty little hole with formica tables and scungy chrome chairs. After we'd got our weasel-piss tea he said, 'My name's Allen,' putting out his huge right hand to shake. 'What's yours?'

'Bet,' I said, grinning at him. He had charisma and was beginning to radiate warmth. I was tingling, attracted even as I shook his hand.

'I'm sorry I stared,' he said. 'It's just that your tits reminded me of my mum.'

'Really?' No man had used this line on me before. 'Still around is she — your mum?'

'No,' he said softly, sadly. 'She died this time last year.' Allen's eyes filled with tears. I put my hand on his. What could I say? I felt sorry for him.

'You have such beautiful breasts. Mum used to wear tops like yours, that's why I was staring. I'm sorry if I offended you.'

'No, you didn't really,' I said, lying valiantly. He stroked my hand, very gently. It was amazing how gentle that huge hand was.

'I'd love it if I could hold you. Just for a while. To feel someone in my arms again,' he begged. I thought — he's sweet. Seems harmless enough — why not? So when we got outside in the warm darkness I let him take me into his arms. His huge body made me tingle with excitement. He smelt . . . wonderful. Compatible somehow . . . like . . . my own brother, or my cat . . . like baby powder and chocolate. He spent ages nuzzling my tits with his face and it felt *sooo* good. I made up my mind that I'd like to sleep with him there and then. His huge hands were firm but gentle on my body, roaming everywhere. I slapped him away only every second time and I started to get really turned on.

We had dinner a few times. I watched him play in the Colts. I loved to see his big strong body running, grabbing the ball, avoiding tackles. God, I even got interested in rugby because he was so good at it. I became more and more turned on by his fixation for my tits and I happily spent time while we were kissing stroking his cock — it was magnificent and I lusted for it. I couldn't sleep at night for dreaming of his body on top of mine and although I had never had a lover before my body knew what it wanted.

A couple of weeks later he took me home. I'd got to know him better, to trust his gentleness. Mum liked him, said he was a good boy, from a good family, what a tragedy it was that his mum had died last year. Allen was an only child. His dad had died years before. He'd lived with his mum since then and now he lived on his own in the only home he'd ever known.

We both knew this was the night for us. To make love for the first time. I'd only had one boyfriend before and he'd just kissed me. Allen hadn't mentioned any girlfriends at all. We felt our virginity acutely. I was trembling all over, half scared, half excited. When we'd had a beer and he'd shown me around the house, just an old four-room farmhouse with the kitchen/bathroom lean-to on the back, he went into the bathroom and began running a bath.

'I'd like you to have a bath,' he said, kissing me lightly. He gently began undressing me. Whenever I tried to help he wouldn't let me so I just stood there grinning and preening as he slid off my blouse, my skirt, panties and last of all my bra. Allen slowly slid his hands all over my breasts and cupped them. They filled his hands. The nipples contracted and he knelt so he could more easily suck on each one. I was almost passing out as he caressed them with his tongue and lips. It was as if there was an electric current passing from his mouth through me to my most intimate parts. Places I longed for his penis to stroke from within.

Then he led me to the tiny warm bathroom full of steam and helped me into the bath. He tenderly washed me all over, pussy, asshole, underarms. He paid particular attention to my breasts, of course, driving me wild with delight as he soaped and tweaked my nipples until I was shuddering and almost coming.

He even washed my hair and massaged my head. It was heaven, surrendering to his big, capable hands. When the washing was finished he dried me off gently, slowly, even between my toes; then he led me to his big new bed which was pulled down with fluffy flannelette sheets and lit by a soft bedside light. Does he really live like this or has he been planning ahead, I wondered.

He gestured to the bed and I lay down. Ready and open for him. Allen rolled me onto my stomach and I felt something cool sprinkle on my back. Then a soft, smooth brushing began. Ahhhhhh . . . What was he doing? I'd never heard of this before. The girls at school had related stories of being spread wide and thrust into right away, hurt, vandalised, virtually raped for their first sex. They hadn't mentioned brushing.

Allen brushed baby talc all over every inch of my skin with a soft body brush until I was shimmering with frustrated desire. Every time I tried to touch his body he avoided me. God I was so wet and aching with need my cunt felt like it would self-destruct in twenty seconds!

Finally he stood up and undressed. Let free that big

cock which stood erect, dripping, longing for me, my cunt; just as I was longing for him.

'Please, please let me suck you, please,' I begged. But he lay on the bed and said, 'Now you brush me.' So I brushed him all over with the baby talc. Every time I tried to satisfy my desire with his body he would stop me. He was so physically strong there was nothing I could do about it. Eventually he lay on his back smiling and lifted me up over him. I was weak with excitement.

He sat me astride his big body and stroked my open cunt with a finger. My juices were everywhere, running over him and down my thighs. He sucked his finger and slid it in for more. Then added another finger. I moved down on his hand while he kneaded my tits with his other. I tried to slide down on his cock but he wouldn't let me. He slowly rubbed my clit, all the time looking deep into my eyes, smiling softly without speaking. Then he slid two huge fingers deep inside me and moved them up and down against my muscles, waited until I was close to fainting, almost ready to explode. Only then did he slide me down his body and his cock vanished deep inside me.

The pleasure was absolutely unbelievable. I came and came, pulsing with fireworks as he fucked me. He was so strong he could lift my body into any position either of us wanted to try. Every few minutes he would change position and in each position he made sure I came. He could even stand, holding me up in the air with my legs around his waist and finally, dripping sweet baby-powdered sweat onto me, he filled me with his come, crying out my name in the most touching, vulnerable way.

Wow! I collapsed. Utterly, utterly fulfilled. Allen had me. Then and there. I'd do anything for more of him, his body, sex with him. We stayed together that night and the next day when we made love I gave him the bath treatment and teased his cock endlessly. I would squeeze it between my big tits, letting him drip pre-come patterns into the powder that covered us both.

He had me play 'mother'. I even learned to put a huge loose nappy on him and powder him and his erection. Then when he'd had enough of being babied by me we'd fuck until we were both exhausted.

Allen made this seem so natural I just joined in without even thinking about it – what it really might mean about him, his relationship with his mum. I loved the way he worshipped my tits. I loved his stamina, the baby powder and brush, his beautiful cock, his kisses and how he made me come over and over again.

It didn't take long for him to reach rugby's first division. I'd stand on the sideline, watching his big strong body following that grubby little oblong ball, and luxuriate in the thought that later I'd bathe and powder him, dress him up in his own special baby clothes and then fuck wildly all night. God, I miss him . . .

♋

Bet looked at her workmates. 'You don't believe me, do you?' she asked, a bit grumpy at the bemused expressions on their faces.

'You're right!' said Sam. 'I sure don't believe that — a rugby forward who wants to be powdered and have nappies put on him before sex! You've got to be joking!' She laughed and shrugged her shoulders.

'Well I'm not!' said Bet hotly. 'What would you know or appreciate about men anyhow? You've only ever fucked women!'

Before Sam could leap in, Tiffany intervened.

'Come on Sam!' she said firmly, warningly, placing her hand on Sam's thigh, patting her leg. 'Why shouldn't we believe Bet? She listens to our stories, no matter how weird they are, and never puts us down about them. How would we possibly know everything about the stuff that turns men on?'

'What I want to know is what happened then,' said Fiona. 'If you were so happy, how come you aren't together now?'

Bet wriggled on her sofa, looked up at the roof, then down at the floor.

'I'm not sure, really. I wanted to marry him but he got interested in politics and never looked back for me. He was ambitious in that direction and I didn't show much interest, I suppose.' She laughed. 'I was more interested in sex! I saw his wedding in the newspaper and the woman he did marry looks almost exactly like his mum. I think she's got bigger tits, though. He met her at a do for the National Party and phoned me up one day to say that he wouldn't be coming home that weekend to see me. That was the last time I heard from him or saw him until today.'

Louise began to laugh. 'This motherfucker is in parliament now, you say?'

Bet wiped her eyes and blew her nose.

'Yeah,' she said softly. 'I'd love to fuck him again. I really would. Maybe he's ruined me. Perhaps I loved him so much I just haven't got time for other men.'

'Well, you haven't found anyone interesting so far and you've been through all our friends, brothers, flatmates and cast-offs. Perhaps you're right!' said Louise.

Tiffany paced around the office. You could virtually hear her brain ticking over as she walked. Finally she stopped beside Bet's chair and said, 'Well, why don't you?'

'Don't I what?' asked Bet, who was dreaming away.

Louise was at her computer and had found a site with photos of all the sitting MPs.

'Here he is!' she shouted 'A real stud, eh? You can't see any baby powder stains on him these days. Come on Bet! Come and see if this is the one.'

Bet gathered her skirts together and went over, her high heels tapping loudly on the rimu floorboards. She brushed her curls away from her face and leaned close over Lou's fragrant shoulder. Cheek to cheek they scanned the pages of elected representatives.

'Yeah,' she said, pointing. 'That's him.' They all gathered around and looked.

'National, eh?' snorted Sam. 'How like a bloke from Invercargill. Could almost be like wearing nappies again on the back bench behind Jenny Shipley!' she hooted with laughter. Everyone giggled except Bet.

'Shoosh, Sam!' said Bet. 'He can't help it! He was sweet and gorgeous once. An orphaned rugby player, not an MP.'

Tiffany was looking at the tall hunk in the black suit on the screen with interest.

'You could e-mail him and ask to meet him, couldn't you? Look. There's an address at the bottom.'

'Why would he want to see me after all these years?'

'Well . . . he's been in Wellington for a year or so flatting on his own. His buxom wife and kids are left behind in that remote South Island electorate. He might just be a bit horny from time to time and it would be difficult to find a woman who loved sex, baby powder and mothering as much as you once did! Most women would want to know why he was into baby shit like that. What do you think?'

'Yeeeesss. Oh God!' Bet exclaimed. 'Just remembering those times is enough to make me wet. But if I did meet him I'd have to be ready for any reaction. Any reaction at all, I suppose.'

Fiona was watching with her arms folded, dreading seeing Bet hurt again. 'You are all really stupid! Let the past be just that. If you want to wank off the thought of him get some baby powder. I bet Sam or Tiff would love to brush it all over you. Give you a few good orgasms to go to bed with. Forget about the guy. Jesus Christ! Just because you were lovers when you were teens means nothing now.'

'Yeah, you're probably right,' said Bet. She stuck her lip out and looked like she was about to cry again. Tiffany put her arm around her, frowning at Fiona.

'Come on! Cheer up! Be a devil! There's nothing to lose. You are old friends, after all. Lou will set up an e-mail and you can send him a prim little message asking for a meeting and suggesting that little café down at the waterfront, what's it called? The Fifties?'

'No — it's Café Victoria now.'

As Bet sat down at Lou's computer she said, 'You know, there was something that really pissed me off about him. What was it? Oh yeah. He always ruined good cooking by plastering it with tomato sauce. I remember one day I'd cooked him this really yummy meal and he never even tasted it. He just plastered it all over with salt and pepper and sauce. I watched him doing that and I thought, I can't stand this for the rest of my life. Baby powder yes, tomato sauce — not.' But she finished the e-mail and sent it.

$\mathcal{M}$arie Antoinette's is the place to be in the city, thought Louise as she waited for Tiffany the next afternoon. The alluring music went well with the rococo reproductions of shepherds seducing milk maids and bronzed plush stools crowded around huge timber-slab tables.

Louise stared at her empty coffee cup as she waited in an alcove at the back of the café. Her heart pumped much too loudly. Adrenalin surged through her body and her hands tingled and sweated.

What does Tiffany want? What's on her mind? God, I feel

so ashamed of being caught like that in front of the computer. I sort of forgot that I wasn't at home. She blushed again at the thought of what she had been doing. But if anyone was to catch me, Tiffany would be the one I'd want.

Dearest Tiffany, Louise breathed, leaning back, stretching her arms above her head. How amazing she is! I remember when we first met in Angel's Gallery . . . ha! What an incredible day that was.

I had gone there to look at the latest installations. I used to like that sort of thing. In the gallery were Fiona and Bet, looking just like twins, wearing matching black sweaters, strangely out of place against the white walls and brightly coloured installations which thrust themselves energetically into the air.

I had gone to see Angel, the owner of the gallery. She is always entertaining, full of fun and nastiness in equal parts. You can always get some deliciously evil gossip about MPs or models, art collectors or playwrights from Angel. She knows them all.

I was disappointed. She wasn't there. Tiffany arrived after me and she was glorious. She had on a red outfit. Beret, tights, mini dress. Her lipstick was the same shade as well. Her long bronze hair hung in tangled curls down her back. I stood behind an installation and stole glances at her as she paced up and down the gallery looking at the art, not as if she was interested in it, just to keep moving, like a tawny lioness.

Tiffany asked me the time. I didn't have a watch. I don't think I even owned one then. She went over to ask Fiona and Bet and they didn't have a watch between them either. I laughed and Tiffany laughed too. 'Why doesn't anyone here have a watch?' she asked. 'What is *with* us?'

'Is it because we are unemployed?' asked Bet, grinning.

'Are you all really unemployed?' asked Tiff as she took us all in.

'Yup — yeah,' we mumbled, shuffling around. It's not easy to admit you can't get a job. Especially when you love clothes, art and food as much as I do.

'Matching jobs and watches!' Tiffany absolutely reeled with laughter. 'What are we?'

'Well — what are you?' asked Fiona, a bit annoyed.

'Tiffany. I'm unemployed too,' said Tiff, holding out her hand, always straightforward. 'I've got some ideas about getting a business together. That's what I wanted to discuss with Angel today. It's typical of her that she's not here. I wonder where Sam is?'

'Who is Sam?' I asked.

'My gorgeous lover,' said Tiffany proudly. 'The most intelligent blonde butch in the world.' We all laughed. But it was true, we discovered later.

'Do you all live in Wellington?' asked Tiffany.

'We do now,' said Bet. 'I'm Bet, from Invercargill, down south, you know, the asshole of the world?' Everyone grinned, not believing it for a minute. 'I came up here looking for a job and got a good one temping down at Parliament House. But then shit happened and now I'm out of work.'

'So what did happen?' I asked sympathetically.

'Ah — the old bitch who ran the temping agency was a lesbian and she got really hot on me, wouldn't leave me alone. So I had to leave. No references either, damn it.'

'Well,' said Tiffany, looking at Bet in her black sweater and lace tights with her dark curls all tousled and damp from the rain outside, 'I can understand why she would lust after you, but surely you could take her to court for sexual harassment, couldn't you?'

'Yeah, maybe,' said Bet, 'but the way she made my life hell would keep on happening if I did that. Better to make a clean break and get out altogether.'

'I left with her. I'm Fiona. From Palmerston North, originally. We're flatmates.' Fiona was slim and plain with straight brown hair and the same taste in black as Bet.

'I'm Louise — Lou for short,' I said. We all hugged hello.

'Damn, where are Sam and Angel?' wondered Tiffany. 'Hey!' she said excitedly. 'This meeting must be meant to be — you know, cosmically speaking. Let's go out and have a meal together. You might be interested in my business proposition! Nope! I'm not going to talk about it yet. Wait till we are having dinner.'

While we waited for Sam and Angel we decided to go to the local Turkish restaurant. There were enough of us to sit under the canopy which hung over the round table with the lovely cushions. The attractive prospect of food and fun and shared meagre purses emerged, glowing, from the grey despair of the dole. Maybe, just maybe, this crazy optimistic woman with the red clothes and amazing hair had a really good idea!

♋

Louise's reverie was interrupted by the waiter asking if she wanted anything else. She shook her head and since Tiffany had still not arrived she dropped back into the memory of their first time together.

♋

Sam and Angel returned, their arms around each other. Tiffany ran to them, hugged them both. 'Where have you been, you bitches?' she demanded cheerfully.

'We were checking out the galleries over the road. They have some real dumb shit in them, you know?' said Angel in a slightly drunk voice. She looked like a fat version of Stevie Nicks. 'Not like in *my* gallery where excellence reigns,' she flourished her arm expansively at the gallery space around her.

'Yeah, and then we went to Queen's for a drink or two,' said Sam, swaying as she leaned possessively into Tiffany. Sam looked like a man, almost sounded like one. Her voice was husky and warm. Most of her head was shaved and it gave her the appearance not of Sinead O'Connor, more the feeling you get seeing a league team walk into a pub — if the guys in a league team ever wore heaps of earrings, black leather T-shirts and pants.

'You are both drunk! It's disgusting!' said Tiffany crossly. 'Look at us, we have been waiting ages for you to turn up. These women here could be wealthy clients wanting to buy a painting, Angel.' She gestured towards Fiona, me and Bet.

'Oh shit! Are you? Do you?' Angel swung away from Sam and wandered to her desk. 'Here's the catalogue!'

'No . . . no,' laughed Bet, waving the catalogue away. 'We'd love to buy some paintings because they're really excellent but we haven't even got enough money for dinner, damn it!'

'I was just joking, Angel,' said Tiffany. 'Why don't you come to dinner and sober up a bit? We are going to the Istanbul — OK?'

'Great!' she said, 'Just let me lock up and I'll be right with

35

you.' Since Angel was more than a bit incapacitated everyone helped her shut up the gallery.

In the restaurant we laughed and joked. Tiffany was into astrology and discovered the amazing coincidence that we had all been born in the same year. 'This meeting *must* be meant to be. It's karmic!' she declared, glowing in her red clothes under the canopy like the Queen of Sheba.

'Here's my idea,' she said enthusiastically when the main courses lay steaming in front of us. 'What I plan is to start a business in the city. A business based around a group of creative people, women even better. I don't know what your skills are but if you like the sort of art that Angel has in her gallery, you don't wear watches and you are all around my age — you are my kind of people.

'So, tell me a bit about yourselves and we will see what sort of skills we can pool together. You start, Louise,' she said, grabbing a pita bread and digging into the food.

'OK . . . ' I said, sipping my wine. 'I am from Thames and I qualified as a travel agent before I met Bill. We moved to Wellington so he could get work. I'm almost three months pregnant to him. Bill is the kind of guy who doesn't want me to work so we are just scrabbling along on his income. I do miss working though and I love computers.' Everyone murmured congratulations and commiserations too.

'Fiona?' asked Tiff. Fiona wriggled on the embroidered

cushions, thrusting her hands up through her short brown hair.

'I started a veterinary degree at Massey but I dropped out after a couple of years. I preferred working and earning money. Seems silly now, but there it is. I am good at marketing stuff. I used to temp in all sorts of businesses and I did a lot of work for advertising agencies.'

'Bet?' asked Tiff

'Well . . . I've done sales work for Toyota. I really enjoyed it until they made me redundant. I love art but I have never had enough money to buy anything yet. I went temping and met Fiona at the agency. She helped me get the courage to leave the last job I was in, where that old bitch hassled me all the time.'

'What about you?' asked Fiona. 'Who are you Tiffany? What about you, Sam?'

Tiffany grinned irrepressibly and looked around everyone as we ate, clearly enjoying the company and the surroundings. 'I'm an arts graduate. From Victoria. Which means I know heaps about things that don't matter in the slightest. I have a lot of business ideas though and . . . I reckon we could put together a good advertising agency between us.' Before we could say anything she added, 'I know, I know. There's lots of competition in the market. But we are all women, and women are naturals at lateral thinking, coping with more than one input at a time, doing lots of things simultaneously. Advertising seems to be like that. I'm amazed men can cope with it, actually.' We all laughed.

'I know what you mean,' I said, 'Bill can't do anything while he's watching TV, he's too busy just doing that. He can't even peel the spuds.'

'I think it's a good idea, Tiffany. I've just finished a small business management course,' said Fiona. 'I think we could set up something really easily but we would have to pool our resources. We wouldn't know if we were going to be successful for a couple of years at least. That's standard, really.'

'Sam — tell them something about you, darling,' said Tiffany.

Sam looked shy for a moment. 'Hi, I'm from Wellington. I have a fine arts degree and I love selling things. But no one wants me in their office because I look too butch. I like leather too much.' She ran her hands over her naked temples and tugged at the piercings which punctured her ear lobes. Tiffany leaned towards her and kissed her cheek. 'I refuse to change the way I want to look for a bunch of suited wankers in a high-rise,' she finished angrily.

'Sam and I discovered each other six months ago,' said Tiffany. Sam put her arm around Tiffany and sat back, looking proud. 'I was fed up with men, anyway,' said Tiffany.

'I've been attracted to women ever since I can remember. I've never had any boyfriends,' said Sam. 'I just got lucky with Tiff. Do any of you feel threatened by us? Being lesbian, I mean?'

Angel squealed. 'Threatened? No – I keep asking to join you and you won't let me!'

Laughing, Tiffany waved her arm lazily at Angel. This was obviously a perennial subject. 'Darling you always chicken out at the last minute. We aren't going to ask you any more.' She kissed Angel on the cheek. Sam leaned over Tiffany and stuck out her tongue lewdly at Angel. 'Any time you need a fuck come to Samantha for a good time, Angel cake.' Her voice was husky and inviting. Angel squealed and said, 'Oooh! You girls!' fluttering her hands at Sam.

Bet frowned but then flushed as she said, 'Well, the last job I had wasn't good for the lesbian reputation but I have to admit . . . Fiona and I *did* try sleeping together. Just to see what it was like.' We all laughed at her discomfort and Sam patted her shoulder.

'It was my fault it didn't work. I'm just too hetero, not really turned on by a body like my own,' explained Fiona.

'I love men too,' I said, thinking of Bill, the exquisite pleasure we had sometimes, though not so often lately. 'But you don't put me off. I envy you. An equal relationship with neither of you calling the shots over the other.'

'Don't you believe it!' laughed Tiffany. 'Sam can be a bossy little butch when she wants! Eh, darling?'

Sam dabbed a sploof of yoghurt on Tiffany's nose and licked it off. Tiffany grinned. 'So where are we at? Fiona's interested, Sam and I are committed to getting off the dole. What about you, Bet?'

'I don't know really. Well — yeah. It would be great to get together and start a business using our expertise. I need a job. I'm quietly starving on the dole.' She did look rather on the thin side.

'Yes,' I said enthusiastically. 'I wasn't really looking for a job but Bill isn't earning enough for us to live on and we have a baby arriving so we need more dough. I'm in if you are!'

'Angel?'

'Hmmmmm. I don't think so darlings. I have my own business. I'm willing to give you my advertising account, for all the good it does you. But I just haven't got the time or the energy to really offer you anything more meaningful.'

'Wow! Our first account! Already!' crowed Tiffany. 'Ladies, a toast to our future success!'

Louise stretched and wriggled in her seat. That was . . . what? Three fabulously successful years ago. She left Bill because of

Tiffany's influence. The silly asshole couldn't stand the thought of her working. It devalued the status of his job in their relationship, he said. Despite the obvious fact that they couldn't make ends meet with his income. Now he had disappeared to Aussie and left her with Sampson.

'God, where *is* Tiffany?' Louise wondered aloud, thinking she would have to get herself another coffee and biscotti soon if Tiffany didn't hurry up.

'Here I am. It's busy today, isn't it?' said Tiffany suddenly, appearing with a glass of wine in her hand. 'Sorry I'm late, parking out there is hell.' She leaned over and kissed Louise on the cheek. 'Do you want another drink?'

'No thanks.' Louise suddenly felt faint, her hands were trembling and she wanted, wanted so very much what she hoped Tiffany was thinking about.

Tiffany sat silently for a while, playing with her wine glass. Abruptly she said, 'I suppose what I want to tell you is that I'm into the sort of bondage and discipline that you are into, Lou. I'd love to do some scenes with you. If you'd like to?' Tiffany's heart beat faster, she felt like she was suffocating. What an awful risk this was! And with one of her business partners too.

Louise blushed and hung her head. Tiffany watched her, how absolutely gorgeous she was. That fine pale skin, long black hair hiding those blue eyes. How much more her beauty would shine if she were sexually fulfilled! For a heady moment Tiffany could see Louise bound and submissive, kneeling at her booted feet. She took a deep breath and gulped her wine then ordered another glass from the slim young man who was one of the regular day staff. He was cute. But probably gay, Tiffany noted in passing.

Leave the boys alone! she reprimanded herself. Just focus on work and the women at Tiffany's. That's enough for any human being, no matter how horny.

Finally Louise said slowly, 'I always thought that stuff was just for the Internet. I never realised that we could do it for real. Can we?'

'Yes. We can,' said Tiffany. 'I have a friend who may hire us one of her dungeons. We could meet there and spend the evening or afternoon. Just try things out. What do you think?'

Louise reached out and clasped Tiffany's hand. Hard. She was trembling. 'Yes,' she whispered, 'Oh yes please!' Marie Antoinette's seemed to shimmer and glow. Tiffany squeezed Louise's hand in return. 'What about Sam? Isn't it being unfaithful to her?' asked Louise.

'Yes. Maybe. Except she isn't into anything except vanilla sex and, frankly, I'm a bit bored with it. Not that I don't love her, but over the years the excitement has worn off and she isn't really interested in experimentation. You and I will have to be really cool about it. You do understand that, don't you?

I really don't want to split with Sam just yet. We have too many things in common.'

'Yes, I know. I am grateful, Tiff, I really am. It gives me something to look forward to.' She lifted Tiffany's hand to her lips and kissed it, shuddering. 'I will do whatever I can to please you.'

Tiffany grinned wickedly, showing her teeth. 'You will. Oh yes, you will sweetheart. Because if you are not very, very good you will be punished severely.' She pulled Louise into the corner of their alcove out of sight of the bar and kissed her mouth very softly, then took Louise's underlip between her teeth and bit sharply down. Louise cried out and tried to pull back but Tiffany wouldn't allow her to. Her hands were wound into that lovely silky hair, holding Louise still.

'Do you still want this?' asked Tiffany intensely. 'Do you? Do you?' Tears filled Louise's eyes and she nodded. Red tooth marks bloomed on her lip and she sucked it in, ran her tongue over her punished flesh.

'Yes,' she whispered. 'I trust you absolutely, Tiffany. Do anything you like with me.'

She's absent-minded again, thought Sam, frowning, watching Tiffany mooning around selecting clothes, attempting to get dressed. Sam pulled up her Levis and tightened the belt around her hips. She had decided to pack a whacker tonight and felt a comforting hard swelling filling the front of her jeans. I enjoy feeling the way a man does, Sam thought, admiring her strong body in the mirror. At her regular work-out at the gym that day Sam had put a heavier weight on the bench-press than she had ever attempted before. Lifted it too. She rippled her muscles in front of the mirror and hoped that Tiffany was watching. Hot floods of pride and possessiveness poured through Sam and erased her pleasure in her profile.

Tiffany was fluffing around in her bra and panties trying to decide what to wear. Sam never thought about clothes much — she wore jeans and T-shirts or bush shirts. There were no dresses in her wardrobe although she loved it when other women wore dresses.

Sam sat down, poured herself a glass of wine and watched Tiffany rummage again through her huge wardrobe of clothes. 'Come ON!' she said finally after Tiffany, with a vacant look in her eyes, had tried on a dozen outfits. 'It's ten already, what's up with you tonight?'

Tiffany looked at Sam and smiled slowly. 'Oh . . . OK. Nothing's up,' she said lightly, seeming to pull herself together.

'Where are we going?' asked Tiffany as they finally went out the door.

'Gorgon's,' said Sam shortly. The taxi had been waiting for at least fifteen minutes and it was her turn to pay.

'Oh!' said Tiffany, sounding put out but not arguing. Sam knew that Tiff didn't like Gorgon's much but Sam wanted to go there tonight. It was the favourite den of her leather-loving pierced friends and she felt at home there. Tiffany had enough personality to enjoy herself anywhere so Sam wasn't worried about her.

As they got out of the taxi the pounding music coursed through their bodies and seemed to make the air pulse around them. They paid and squeezed past the huge doorman who bounced for Gorgon's. He had on an enormous T-shirt with a medusa head emblazoned front and back. His wild black dreadlocks set off the whole effect.

Sam found her friends hidden away in their usual dark corner of the nightclub. She snuggled in and began catching up on the latest gossip. Tiffany said hi to everyone, shared around kisses and hugs and then an irresistible rhythm buried in the disco noise took her out onto the dance floor.

She's absent, absent without leave. What, or rather *who* is she thinking about? Sam watched jealously as Tiff flung her gorgeous body around inside the fluid fabric she was wearing; spinning and leaping under the disco lights. I've never seen her like this before, I wonder what it is all about?

She went out to dance with Tiffany, pressing her jeans up against Tiffany's backside, sliding her hands over the silky fabric, feeling slick muscles moving under the skin, the warmth of lust flowing through her body. Tiffany undulated against Sam but didn't look at her or respond. Sam realised she wasn't wanted and slipped back into the corner where she kept an eye on Tiffany to make sure another woman didn't hit on her or a man try the same.

Not seeing Sam leave her, responding instead to another

vision inside her head, Tiffany danced. Sam had ceased to be there and Louise was her partner instead. The music drowned out feeling and thought, the bass notes throbbing round her heart.

♋

Sweet submissive Louise knelt naked at her feet. Mistress Tiffany was dressed head to foot in soft black worn leather. She wore her best black high-heel boots for Louise. Tiffany ruffled Louise's long silky dark hair with the tip of her riding crop.

'Mistress . . .' whispered Lou, 'Mistress . . . punish me, I am a very bad girl. I have let you down this week. I lusted after you and I came without your permission on Wednesday.' Her head drooped down towards Tiffany's boots. Tiffany moved her stance slightly, bracing her legs strongly. She leaned down and grabbed the black collar around Louise's neck by the loop at the back and dragged Louise between her spread legs. She gripped Louise's face between her knees and stared down at her.

'Kiss my boots, slave!' she hissed and immediately Louise began kissing and licking Tiff's dusty boots. While her boots were getting cleaned Tiffany looked at the spread of Louise's bottom, how delicate, soft and curved and yet generous it was. The whip twitched in her hand and she began to smack Louise's ass cheeks with the flat of the whip, each stroke leaving a red mark and causing Lou to gasp as she kept on licking.

As the spanking went on Louise's cunt got wetter and wetter until she was dripping down her thighs.

'Stop!' ordered Tiffany, wet herself with desire at the sight of Louise's arousal reflected in the mirror on the opposite wall. 'Now, get up on that table.' Louise lay back with her legs wide apart . . .

'Helloooooo . . .Tiffany?' Someone was standing in front of her waving their fingers, trying to get her attention. Reluctantly Tiffany left her dream of Louise and found herself standing in the middle of the darkened dance floor with Mary, an old friend, laughing at her. Somehow the music had faded away.

'Where's Sam?' asked Tiffany.

'I don't know,' said Mary. 'She was here but you just ignored her so she went next door to Rufus's club. You know, where all the naughty boys hang out.'

Tiffany frowned. 'Why would she go there?'

Mary shrugged. 'Search me. Probably bored with you. You have been jiggling around out here for hours. What's going on? Are you on something?'

'Oh —' Tiffany felt embarrassed. 'Just dreaming.' Yes, she said to herself, Louise is my new drug. 'I better go and find Sam I guess, apologise for my behaviour. Thanks Mary.'

5

$\mathcal{L}$ouise sat in Marie Antoinette's for a long time after Tiffany had gone back to work. She stared at her coffee cup and Tiffany's wine glass. She thought about visiting a *real* dungeon. And with Tiffany. Oh God. Her heart pumped. She felt like she'd run and run and run away from her real self all her life. Now by promising to go to a dungeon to do a scene with Tiffany she was falling into the arms of a strong woman, the object of so many of her fantasies. A woman who had always understood her and supported her in all the shit that had gone down over the last few years. 'Dearest Tiffany . . .

How lucky I am,' she breathed, leaning back, hugging herself.

She floated on air all that evening. Sampson was tired and grizzled as he ate his tea. She didn't mind. Was having him a mistake? His chubby three-year-old body slumped in the chair. 'No, Sampson,' she kissed his dark curls, 'my sweet darling boy, your daddy was a mistake but not you.' She read him a bedtime story about a caterpillar and what it ate each day. He was asleep by the time she tucked him in.

In her study she turned on the computer and logged onto the Net. She collected her e-mail and found one from Bet thanking her for finding Allen on the parliamentary website.

'Shit what have we begun?' exclaimed Louise. She thought for a moment and then began an e-mail to Tiffany. 'I do hope Tiff collects her mail tomorrow,' Louise worried to herself. 'Should I phone her? Nah, she's out with Sam clubbing tonight. They always do that on a Friday night. I'll wait till Monday.'

Putting her worries aside she booted up Netscape and began to surf for her favourite naughty sites to prepare herself for an evening lovemaking with herself. Very soon she found that site again, the one Tiffany had caught her in, and began to scan the pictures. Louise smiled and pulled her dressing gown aside, her hand straying over her nipples as she surfed. The dominant women became Tiffany. Louise was the submissive heroine of each sequence. She felt the

51

ropes cut into her, the clips pinch her, the gags fill her mouth. She smiled happily, thinking that her new reality included kinky sex like this. With the gorgeous Tiffany. She sighed in bliss.

It's still my biggest secret, thought Louise, my love affair with the Internet. Even Tiffany doesn't know about it. She might suspect after catching me yesterday but it wouldn't occur to her that the Internet has been keeping me fulfilled all this time when I haven't had a lover.

When I'm horny it has become an utterly erotic thing for me. It gives me what real life has not. Not yet. I suppose I'm actually a control freak. I love seeing only what I want to see; I love ignoring the ads, tuning to what I am in the mood to look at instead of being fed any old ratshit thing at any time which is all the telly does. TV doesn't do anything for me any more. It certainly doesn't have any sex that turns me on. And if they have bondage or S&M in a movie it is always the baddies who get to do the kinky sex. Never the goodies. I hate that. Why can't the goodies have great sex too? They are allowed to kill and that is illegal — sex isn't illicit, is it?

I guess the only thing that disappoints me about the Internet is that no one shows penises erect for the delight of women. And I have hardly ever found a naked woman exhibiting herself for me, another horny woman who loves the female body. If I want to see a hard cock I have to visit gay male sites where they have endless photos of men with gorgeous cocks showing off for each other and if I want to see a woman's wet cunt I have to visit sites, again made for men, to see gorgeous pussy spread wide — but not for my female sex to enjoy. So the guys can wank all over their keyboards and gum them up.

The 'lesbians' are laughable. You can tell they are just doing it for the money, not even for lust. They're bored with it really. Men can't seem to see the difference between lust and boredom on a woman's face. Maybe they don't care?

What have men got that we women don't? I like sexy pictures as much as any male who has ever bought a *Penthouse* or *Playboy*. I wait for a hot photo to download and put myself into the scene with the woman or man. Smell the smell of their sweat, their sex, the perfume of lust, run my tongue up her long neck or down his long prick. Suck her fingers, nipples and tease her cunt lips . . . she sighed aloud. 'Yeah.'

At least I have decided that I *do* like sex with women more than sex with men. Bill was your average 'slam-bam-thank-you-ma'am' kinda guy except he failed to say thanks most of the time. I have watched Tiffany and Sam for years now. The love and respect they share, the touching and tenderness. How they don't put each other down, I hunger for that. I have never found it, maybe I will never find it.

Then recently I discovered that these bondage pictures with a mistress and slave girl really turn me on.

When I get really horny, instead of going out wasting my time looking for a lover I sit here and have a lovely sex session with myself. Mmmmmm, I love it.

Louise left the screen and went to run the bath. She prepared slowly, gradually, for her session at the computer. She squirted perfumed oil into the water and got in. Found the soap and stroked soapy bubbles all over her sweet firm tits, massaging her nipples until they were erect. Squeezing them gently, running her nails over her nipples, then massaging them firmly again.

Already I am imagining that Mistress Tiffany is ordering me to wash myself thoroughly for tonight's session with her. So I soap my fur and slip my fingers between my cunt lips. Already I am wet and slippery inside. Mistress would call me a slut if she saw that. But I am always expected to be wet and ready for her.

When you are a slave you can never win. MMMmmmm yes, it's how I like it. Sort of like being born a sinner. Mistress is like God and knows everything about me and if she doesn't know then she suspects the worst. I am very afraid of her and what she might do to me tonight. Fear makes me even wetter.

Imitating mistress I tease my clit with my fingertip very softly, wondering what new lewd bodies will be on the Net tonight. Will it be a slim, taut Asian girl? Or a golden woman with a blond Swedish hunk impaling her on his huge erection because mistress has ordered my humiliation with a male lover? What will I find? The mystery is so exciting.

I stroke oil onto my body after the bath. Mistress always likes me naked before a session so she can inspect me thoroughly all over. She will order me to dress later, so I grab my satin robe.

Sampson is asleep; no one else is at home. Tonight I will be totally wicked. My nipples are erect and between my legs is slick, simmering. In the bedroom I open a secret cupboard and pull out my collection of sex toys. Little balls on a string . . . a big black rubber dildo . . . a massager vibrator . . . nipple clips with chains on them . . . lube . . . a butt plug . . . cotton ropes.

Crouching before the cupboard my cunt is wide open, pulsating. Longing for a cock, a spanking, a tongue, anything. I tease it with the cold tip of the dildo and sparkles of pleasure run through me. Groaning I gather up all my wicked things and take them to my computer room where I have a big comfy sofa arranged in front of the screen – not my usual erect office chair.

On the screen is a picture of the last really appealing photo I found on the Net: a brunette woman sucking a huge cock, a big dark hand twined in her hair pulling the nape of her neck most pleasurably taut. I want to kneel before her and suck on her right breast, smell the sweet aroma of her sweat, hear her sucking and the sound of her breathing stopping and starting again as that big pole slides down her throat and up again. I want to reach down between her legs and slip my forefinger between her cunt lips and slide it up and down her slit until she's as wet as I am.

I log onto the Net. I'll go to Persian Kitty to begin with. She's got hundreds of porn links on her site. Shall I take Amateur? Or Professional? One thing I do know, I'm not going to pay for anything. Men can pay for sex but me, never. Maybe that's why they never make pages for me? Ha! Well I don't care!

I like amateur photos more because many of the women have not been shaved and I don't really like artificially bare vulvas — they're for men who fancy little girls I reckon. I'd hate to be shaven myself because my skin is so sensitive and I can't see how it improves the appearance of my sex to make it painfully naked and scratchy. The amateur women who have their masters or mistresses photograph them are proud of themselves. Or they are real slaves being humiliated in front of the camera. I like the thought of that, too.

I surf and slip down and in, in and down, through many pages until I find one with the most gorgeous American girls on it . . . wow . . . just hints of wet through transparent panties . . . Oh yum . . . Oummmm . . . Yeah. I lift up my right leg and start to tease my clit with a feather-light touch. If I do it left-handed it is slightly more difficult and makes the journey longer.

I taste the juices of my body and imagine those lovely girls allowing me to taste theirs. What would they taste like? A little like me, I suppose. When I am tired of gazing at velvet thighs and pouting lips I find a page with breasts on it. I love small-to-average breasts. Small breasts are lovely to cup in your hands, take that nipple between your lips, stroke the tip ever so slowly with your tongue. I can see the sweet woman on the screen wink at me. I want to take her hand and pull her out of the screen towards me, have her land astride my lap, her wet cunt pressed naked against mine, her breasts pressed against me.

I will brush my mouth over her full-budded lips and squeeze her ass cheeks apart, snuggle her in closer and closer still, her tongue inside my mouth, my hands kneading her back and bum and slipping ever nearer, nearer her lovely asshole. I want to feel that moist little hole and ease my finger into it as I slowly rub her clit with my other hand.

She moans softly and then louder and louder. The sounds of pleasure she makes arouse me further. I want to feel her body contract and arch around me as my deft fingers make her come.

I take the cold lube and anoint the butt plug with it. I slowly anoint my asshole with lube. Then, stroking that sensitive little hole of mine, I look for an ass with something up it. A cock, a dildo, a row of ivory balls, ahhhh . . . it takes a while but I have all night.

At last I find what I really want to see. A lovely black woman leaning backwards over the edge of the bed with her legs wide, thrusting a huge dildo up her ass. I can see how wet she is . . . how she loves it . . . as I do.

I want to be there for her, to thrust it in and out for her and suck on her clit at the same time. To have her strap on a huge dildo and thrust into my asshole. To recklessly fuck me with her breasts tossing wildly, a butt plug up her bum at the same time. I ease the big plug up . . . Ahhhhhh. O God! I almost came.

I sit, panting, throbbing. I decide to switch to the gay male pages. I'm looking for a huge cock with a big knob and until I find it among all the advertising and crap I will chill out and try to get used to that huge rubber pole up inside my sensitive colon.

Distended, restrained, my cunt drools like a baby teething for a big rusk . . . My clit stands out, longing to be touched. I refuse to touch it . . . NO . . . NO!

Not till I find just the right picture . . . I look for half an hour or more. I flick through page after page finding nothing much until I locate a scene shot around a pool table. Ten men with huge erect penises ready to service each other in turn. The first man is kneeling on the table, his ass over the edge and in the next shot I see that first big cock entering his asshole. Oh . . .! Oh!

I'm so very wet. I look at that photo and imagine those guys taking me alternately with that man on the table. Our ecstatic bodies side by side being fucked hard. I switch back to the black woman. I allow myself to strum my clit slowly, maddeningly slowly . . .

Tiffany and Mary went into Rufus's club. It was full of men, ugly to gorgeous, all looking for a suitable screw for the night or, failing that, a few shared drinks. Tiffany wandered around, trailed by Mary, looking everywhere for Sam. They searched the *hiz* and *mz* toilets, visited the café, stood on the dance floor soaking up male pheromones looking for a zebra-striped croptop. Finally Tiffany asked the bouncer who said, 'Yeah. I saw her, if it was a woman. I thought she was a man with heaps of earrings and punk hair. She left with another woman, a blonde. Gorgeous young chick. Fancied her myself.' Tiffany was stunned. Her Sam! Walked out with another woman! What! Tears in her eyes, she stumbled to the bar and sculled a couple of brandies. None of the men spoke to her and she felt as if she were on an island, lost and alone.

Now it came down to it she had gotten to rely on Sam. To rely on her strong possessive presence beside her. She couldn't take it in. O God! The agony struck viciously. Sam, gone for the night with another woman. Shit.

Floating from the effects of drink and shock Tiffany turned and noticed Mary hovering beside her. Focusing with difficulty she said, 'Thanks for keeping me company, Mary. I'll get a taxi home.'

Mary looked sad. 'Can't I come home with you? I've fancied you for a long long time . . .' Tiffany looked at Mary. A sweet woman friend, no doubt. But not the sort for her, never had been, never could be. She shook her head and hugged Mary, trying to be kind.

'Sorry love. I'm not handling Sam disappearing and I don't feel in the least sexy. Better luck next time you come out – eh?'

'Not even when Sam's gone off with a young thing?' begged Mary.

'No.' Tiffany felt ashamed of herself. Lusting for Louise all night and now turning down Mary. But the feeling just wasn't there. She felt guilty too . . . somehow she had driven Sam away, by ignoring her . . . maybe she had ignored Sam before but tonight it had had a different outcome. She felt sick with fear and loneliness as she walked up the path to their cottage tucked away in a bush-clad valley.

She dodged under the flowers from the wisteria and let herself into the house.

Silence. She checked the whole place. No Sam. She made a cup of coffee and cried hopelessly into a teatowel. On the teatowel a baroque scroll asked, 'Why is lemon juice mostly artificial ingredients but dishwashing liquid contains real lemons?'

♋

Louise got up and made a cup of coffee. Putting off her orgasm further she telephoned Jude.

Jude is the girlfriend I most fancy sexually. Next to Tiffany, that is. I often phone her when it's late and our kiddies are in bed. For half an hour we talk about our kids, school, the garden and the weather while my cunt aches for satiation, for my come, for me to finally give my sex permission to come. Eventually we say goodbye.

Cooled off I go back to the computer with the gang scene still up on the screen. I stand with my legs wide apart and ever so slowly I slide that big dildo into my dripping cunt.

It feels so good I can barely stand up. How I would love Tiffany to be licking me now while I am tied up! With ropes holding my knees wide apart, my swollen sex open and exposed to whoever wants to look. Mmmmm . . . or I'd love that muscular guy there to fuck me while I protested and struggled to get away. All those horny men there to fuck me in turn. Then I'd get to watch them fuck and suck each other.

Ah! What a beautiful thing it is to see two men actually loving each other. I always feel sad for those guys who say their best buddies were the guys they fought alongside in a war somewhere. Humans shouldn't need to be bombed to be friends.

I thrust the dildo in and out. In and out of my body. It feels wonderful but not as good as a real cock. I'm longing for a cock up me, thrusting away from the right angle where it feels best and for a sweet cunt to sit on my face, suffocating me with juices and warm sensitive softness . . .

I strum my clit softly and fast till I almost come and then I stop.

I slide the butt plug out and wash it in cold water. I sit in front of the computer and tease myself again with my fingers and the fat dildo, sliding it in and out.

Then, feeling an unstoppable orgasm rushing upon me, I switch to the photo of the woman on the bed and bury my face in her wet cunt as I come. Stars sparkling around me, I cry out, coming and coming. Struck by lightning, dying from sensory overload and lack of a lover. Ahhh — the release of tension. I flop on the sofa. Exhausted.

Someone knocks on the door. Calls out, 'Hi . . . Lou? Are you awake?' O God — it's . . . It's Tiffany!

Damn! Here I am, just come all over the place, dildo lying on the floor, stuff everywhere, exotic pictures on the computer, a picture of debauchery and I'm ashamed of my secret lusts. Again. Shit. I scramble to my feet. Shout, 'Just a minute!' and shove the dildo under the sofa. Shut down the browser on the computer, pull my dressing gown around me, tie the belt tight — I don't want to offend her, have her think I was being unfaithful to her. And sort of pulled together although wet, sweaty, oily and tousled, I open the door. Tiff's standing there, leaning against the security door looking tired and sad.

'Long time no see.' I grin at her and hug her. 'Didn't you say you and Sam were going out tonight?'

'Yees . . . ' she says sort of sheepishly, sadly too, coming in and shutting the door. 'I just felt I had to see you, Lou. I've got some news.' Tiffany walked quickly across the living room and back again. Finally she looked me in the eye and said, 'Sam's gone off with another lover.'

'What?' I'm incredulous. 'How come?'

Tiffany explains about what happened at the nightclub and afterwards. 'I went home but it was too lonely. I keep

63

thinking of her fucking that blonde bitch and I'm just *so* jealous.' I smile at her and hug her. I hope she can stand the smell of me. She smells gorgeous, always wears some lovely Indian perfume, maybe it's her deodorant. I haven't really asked. Could it be just the odour of her skin . . .? I begin to get wet again thinking of her skin.

'Tiffany, how can you be jealous when you admit you were thinking of me all the time? It was probably instinct that led Sam to wander away and find someone else.'

'Oh — I dunno!' Tiffany cries, grabbing a tissue and mopping her eyes. 'I just *am* jealous! I've put up with Sam's butch jealousy and possessiveness for years. I thought I'd have a fight when you and I eventually brought our relationship out in to the open and now *this* happens.'

As I make us some coffee I gaze at her lovely face. Those soft lips, the way her neck curves as the light outlines her. The way her long dark wavy reddish hair lies around her face and shoulders. I want you, I love you Tiffany, I tell myself. Now's not the time to tell her though. I look Tiffany in the eyes. She looks right back at me. I look down. My face flushes all over and down to my breasts. God. I want her.

Tiffany moves close to me and cups my face in her hands. 'Look at me,' she whispers. 'Look at me.' I look up, right into those big brown eyes full of tears. Then her sweet soft lips are on mine, her tongue stroking my upper lip, her hands undoing my gown, her teeth clumsily clashing with mine, as if we have both forgotten how to kiss. The scent of her body flows over me and I'm away, drugged. The fairies have visited me and I'm their tool. A fool, to lust for my best friend when she's lost her partner like this. I'm a dumb bitch on heat. She's taken control of us. Oh I want her to take control.

Tiffany is stroking my breasts, just the way I love it. She's kissing me and running her tongue maddeningly around my lips. Suddenly she nips my top lip in the centre and tears pour from my eyes at the pain. 'That's because I want you so much, Louise,' she hisses at me. 'Because every bit of pain I give you hurts me too.' I am weak with desire. I am hers.

She orders me to lift off her blouse. We slip her tights off together. I kneel and reverently lower her panties and there . . . in all the beauty I imagined is her lovely . . . ooooooh sweet wet cunt. I can smell her. She's deliciously hot too. I feel guilty, exhilarated. I want to serve her, serve my mistress to the best of my ability.

I press my face into Tiff's soft dark pubes and smell her. She presses onto my face and I part her lips with my fingers trembling and press my nose into her clit. Stick out my tongue and taste her salty softness.

'Sam . . .' she whispers, 'oooo Sam. Lick me, Sam.'

'Tiffany,' I whisper, 'I'm not Sam.' I lick her sweetness some more and then, suddenly, she sat up. Closing her knees.

Putting her head in her hands Tiffany cries, tears falling between her fingers and dripping onto her legs.

'I'm sorry! I can't – we can't do it yet, Lou. I just can't. Not until I know what's happening with Sam.'

I get my coffee and sip it, feeling really lonely and sad. 'I understand, Tiff. I really do,' I say. 'You'd better go home and I'll go to bed. Oh – and read your e-mail tomorrow. I remembered something that Bet told me once.'

*I*nside the taxi Sam looked down at Daniella. How sweet! Such a sexy, flirtatious, young and innocent girl. Sam felt strong, masculine, experienced, protective – and very aroused by Daniella. All the things she no longer felt towards Tiffany, she now realised. Damn it! Sam could see their relationship swirling down the drain because Tiffany had happened to have an off night and Sam couldn't resist this delicious young thing.

Her blood pressure rose as Daniella's soft little paw with pearl-painted nails crept into her hand . . . ahhhhhh . . . what a delight she was!

Sam had wandered into the neighbouring nightclub, bored with watching Tiffany getting off on her own, dancing like she was a ghost instead of the hot-blooded woman she usually was for Sam.

Once on the dance floor she saw Daniella, writhing like a bag of snakes to the music. Her immense and glowing sex appeal meant that there were several men dancing attendance on her. Sam watched them getting her drinks, attempting to kiss her, being charmingly but firmly rebuffed. Sam's eyes travelled appreciatively up and down the delightfully outrageous femme outfit Daniella had chosen for the night.

She was breathtaking in a silver leather mini skirt, diminutive bra under a silver mesh T-shirt, matching mesh stockings and insanely high-heeled shoes. Big blue eyes hidden under a blonde mop of curls. Vivacious smile with beautiful teeth. After trying unsuccessfully to pull her eyes away while Daniella charmed everyone, Sam moved in, cutting a path through the men hovering around with her wide leather-clad shoulders, smiling her wickedest smile and gruffly beginning to talk to Daniella.

The disco was pumping so loud Sam had to put her cheek next to Daniella's for most of the evening and now and then, apparently to change position, she rested her hand on Daniella's stockinged thigh. Just to help the conversation along. When Daniella didn't push Sam away, Sam knew she was in. Her heart beat faster and inside her jeans she became wet around the rubber dildo nestled there.

They laughed a lot and knew the same jokes . . . Daniella seemed very willing to do and try anything as they danced to the slowest beat of the DJ pumping up the club. Daniella effortlessly parted her slim thighs and shimmied over Sam's leg. Sam grinned down at Daniella and lightly stroked her back. Then Sam pressed her tightly into her T-shirt and leather-clad breasts.

Inevitably Sam couldn't resist cupping Daniella's buttocks in her hands . . . she almost fell apart in surprise as Daniella showed her enthusiasm by moving in even closer, rubbing against the big hard erection in Sam's pants. Sam was enjoying Daniella's arousal and thanked her stars she had decided to pack it tonight. She would make sure she didn't disappoint Daniella in any way. As Sam was smiling down at Daniella while they danced crotch to crotch, Daniella whispered, 'Let's go home to my place. Please?' Sam melted immediately. The only word on her mind was 'yes'.

Now Sam couldn't wait to get to Daniella's flat. She planned to pick her up and carry her to the bed. Sam could see it now, those sweet pearly breasts with pink nipples waiting to be sucked and bitten. Her firm flat stomach, those lovely silky tight buttocks, her soft lips melting into Sam's over and over again . . . and dessert . . . that lovely little blonde pussy between shy velvet thighs.

'Mmmmmmm,' Sam murmured as Daniella seemed to read her mind and snuggled into Sam's leather jacket.

'You are so strong! So handsome, Sam!' Daniella sighed softly. Sam buried her mouth in the blonde curls clustered against her chest and inhaled Daniella's delicious smell. New, intoxicating, exciting. Like the first taste of icecream after months on a diet. Sam closed her eyes and tightened her arms around Daniella. This is the woman for me, Sam thought. I don't know what I will tell Tiffany. I hadn't planned being unfaithful to her but . . . oh well . . . what the hell. We'll sort it out.

Daniella leaned against Sam's firm erection and lusted for it. She loved a man who could stay erect. What was his name? Sam, that's right . . . Sam. Short for Samuel. She saw herself kneeling in front of those Levis unzipping the brass zipper, smelling the musky scent of his testicles . . . ahhh sweat and lust oozing out . . . and then eagerly serving that penis with her mouth. She loved to taste come in her mouth. A lovely sweet tingling sensation . . . lots of protein – yum yum. And to think that his groans of ecstasy were caused by her hot hungry mouth! She grinned in the dark as the taxi turned into her street.

Sam was in for a surprise but – he'd forgive her – they

always did. She looked forward to his amazement and her eventual punishment. She sighed happily as she lay against Sam's strong chest and his hands slid up under her mesh shirt to find her nipples and gently stroke them. Home! Here we come, Daniella sang to herself as Sam paid the driver.

Sam stood at the windows looking out while Daniella got ready. She was getting changed into some frilly girl's thing. Sam would soon get her out of that! Daniella's taste was OK, though. Her home was a high-rise apartment with a panoramic view of the southern side of the harbour.

'Here I am!' trilled Daniella. Sam turned around and grinned hungrily. Daniella had changed into the sweetest pink babydoll nightie with frilly panties. A filmy negligee and feathered slippers to match set off her lovely clear skin. Sam paced over the floor towards her, growling in her throat. Daniella gave a little shriek and allowed Sam to chase her around the apartment before getting caught in Sam's strong arms.

Lifting her onto the bed Sam smothered Daniella's face with kisses. Her soft little mouth replied with surprising strength. Sam stripped off Daniella's negligee and nightie and rubbed her face all over Daniella's tiny plump breasts. She began to eagerly lick and suck as Daniella squealed in delight and hurried to undo Sam's jacket. Sam continued to kiss and luxuriate in Daniella's skin, down the stomach, under her arms, then Sam rolled her over and kissed her buttocks rapturously, slowly pulling her panties down.

It was really difficult to get Sam's heavy zippered jacket off but Daniella eventually achieved it and revelled in the rippling muscles she could feel under Sam's T-shirt. She buried her nose in Sam's shirt and smelled her strong sweaty body. Mmmmahhhh. Now for Sam's jeans.

His penis leapt out eagerly, as good quality rubber does, and Daniella sucked at it eagerly, thinking, 'Hmmmmm . . . tastes a bit rubbery . . . I wonder if he has a condom on already?' She slid her slim fingers under Sam's cock, searching for his testicles. They weren't there. Instead she touched warm wet fur and soft silky flesh.

At the same moment Sam let her fingers stray inside Daniella's panties and found, to her surprise, a small, erect and eager penis companioned by a pair of snug naked testicles surrounded by the delicate perfumed blond bush Sam had visualised ever since she set eyes on Daniella.

She grunted in surprise and pulled away from Daniella. 'You're a boy!' she cried incredulously. 'A bloody *BOY*!'

Daniella sat up, tasting her fingers . . . 'And *you* are a woman! I thought you were a man!' She was so surprised she squeaked. 'I only like men!'

'Hah — well get this! *I* only like women!' growled Sam. 'Shit! I can't believe it. How could you possibly attract me? A male? I've *never* wanted a man, not ever!'

Daniella looked scared . . . she pulled her panties up over the now flaccid penis. 'I — I'm gay, really. I am only ever turned on by strong blond macho men with big hard cocks. Men who look like you! I wanted to suck you off, have your big hard prick inside me! I'm a girl in a male body, really I am.' She began to cry. Just like a girl, Sam noted as she sat on the side of the big bed, elbows on her knees, scowling at the floor.

Daniella sobbed into the pillow and Sam felt bad. Really bad. Who knows what it would be like, screwing a girl with a penis? Sam had been a lesbian ever since she could remember and knew nothing of men. They had never interested her. She lay down beside Daniella and awkwardly put her arms around those slim shuddering shoulders, drew him into her body and began to stroke him, wordlessly rocking him, getting accustomed to his maleness, to his having a penis. Shit! No vagina either! Confusion charged around in her mind.

It was so horribly difficult. A part of her wanted to walk out right then and there. She felt humiliated by Daniella, real name Daniel, she assumed. She heard in her head all the laughter at men's expense, the nasty sexist jokes, the horror stories women had told her about their experiences with men. Her vision of men was a simple one and did not include the possibility of a man looking or acting like Daniella.

Sam held Daniella away, looked at him, really looked closely. Those long blonde curls, clear fair skin, lovely plump but admittedly flat breasts. Those shapely long legs, painted fingernails and toes . . . what a sexy feminine package! Hotter to trot than many lesbians she could name. Combined with her innocent youthfulness and her wicked worldly wiseness — no wonder all the men were flocking around Daniella at the club.

He must live as a woman all the time, thought Sam wonderingly. She turned on the bedside lamp. Daniella's bedroom seemed to be arranged as a woman might lay out a very feminine room. A boudoir in fact.

Then Sam thought of herself. How she had adopted classic male clothes and behaviour because it suited her. It seemed so much easier and more honest than the usual frilly silly-girl stuff women were into. This and the fact that she loved to fuck with a strap-on dildo, in fact did everything that she imagined a man would do with a woman and more. Didn't this mean that she and Daniella were the same? Both masquerading as something they really weren't?

Daniella slowly stopped crying. She began to enjoy Sam's closeness, her warm strong arms around her. That hard cock was still there. Why? If Sam was a woman, why a cock? Did dykes really like penises too?

'Do you still want me?' Daniella asked shyly, tremulously.

Sam looked at Daniella for a long moment. 'Yes! damn it!' she said, grinning ruefully. 'I'm wet and damn hard wanting you — I have to admit it. You are the cutest, sexiest thing I have met in ages. Male or female.'

'And you're really muscular and have a big hard cock,' whispered Daniella. 'I'd like to try sex with you. I have never fucked with a woman before.'

'Give it a try, shall we?' asked Sam grinning.

'Yes, please.' whispered Daniella. Her giggles were softened by Sam's mouth which went slowly on to suck gently on Daniella's sweet little penis and testicles and then invaded her sweet smelly bum. Mmmmmm, thought Sam, there's no wet lips but she tastes as good as a woman. Better than some I've had.

Sam's hips bucked her jeans down to her knees as she slid her penis into Daniella's eager hungry mouth. She angled it so her clit was rubbed just the right way as Daniella pulled and sucked. Soon the crescendo of pleasure built and built into a clifftop which Sam flew off with a cry like a seabird coming home.

Relaxing beside Sam on the bed, Daniella realised that Sam's orgasm hadn't been any different to that of the men she had sucked off before. She smiled delightedly, knowing that Sam was not going to go limp like the average man would from coming. When she had her breath back they could go on to more and more fun. Maybe sex with a woman was worthwhile after all?

Sam stood up, switched the bedside light on, adjusted her jeans and pressed her penis out of the brass zipper of her jeans. 'On your knees, deceiving little slut!' she commanded, gesturing to Daniella. He hurried to kneel in front of Sam on the bed with his bottom up in the air. Sam looked at Daniella's trembling body, waiting to be serviced and luxuriated in her power . . . how sweet and helpless this man – this woman – is. For a male he's a damn good woman. Let's see how he reacts to a bit of punishment.

'You deceived me! For that I am going to give you a good spanking!' announced Sam loudly and commenced lightly spanking Daniella's sweet little bottom. Daniella squealed and panted as her cheeks became rosy pink. Suddenly she cried out and Sam noticed that Daniella had come all over the bed in front of her.

'You messy little girl, Daniella, coming everywhere like that. Now I am going to fuck you!' Sam said in a her loudest, deepest voice, sliding a condom onto her penis and reaching for the lubricant. Daniella had a huge tube of lube sitting, most ungirlishly, on her bedside table. My whacker has never had this sort of treatment before, Sam thought as she looked at Daniella's slim body and slowly rubbed her hard penis up and down Daniella's crack. Exploring, feeling that soft dimpled asshole. Slowly, forcefully pushing in — in to that willing loving body . . . ahhhh . . .

Daniella opened up and let Sam in. They both cried out together in ecstasy. Sam picked Daniella up, holding her close as she slowly pumped in and out of Daniella. Their mouths met hungrily. Sam reached around and began to softly stroke Daniella's cock, just as she would stroke Tiffany's clit when they fucked in the same position. Soon Daniella came again, crying her pleasure into Sam's mouth.

Sam felt suddenly at one with this tiny man/woman. A she/male. Sam felt the world turn aside, flip over like an aerobatic aeroplane . . . she fell over onto the bed with Daniella still impaled and held tight to her. 'Oh Goddess,' Sam whispered. 'I think I love you, Daniella. Oh Goddess . . . oh my Goddess . . .'

Sam woke from sleep to find that her penis had been removed and Daniella was ensconced between her legs, licking as expertly as Tiffany had ever licked, at Sam's erect clit, sucking and drinking her juices, aroused earlier and still swamping her cunt. Sam moaned in pleasure, lifted her hips higher and parted her legs more. Daniella had lit some candles in glittering glass sconces and set them around the bed. Her blonde curls glowed like a halo, cascading down to mix with the dark curls Sam grew when she wasn't bleaching her hair.

Sam came again, crying out 'Daniellaaaa —
ahhhhhhhhhh!' shuddering as that unrelenting tongue sent
her over the edge into ecstasy once more. Then she felt
Daniella sliding up her, biting tiny bites around her navel,
arousing her interest once again. Moving up Sam's body,
sucking on her hard nipples. As breasts they were nothing
much, more pec than tit, she always said. But they made up
for their small size with extreme sensitivity and she moaned
softly as Daniella's mouth nibbling and sucking sent her
heavenward once more. Daniella rubbed her tiny pink
nipples against Sam's firm breasts, looking deep into Sam's
eyes. Her face was dewed with perspiration and her smile
filled the sky.

And then Sam was intrigued. What was Daniella doing
with her hand? She felt it slide into her hot wet vagina. O
God! It felt so wet, hot and tingly, so wonderful . . . so
delicious . . . 'Ahhhhhhh,' Sam moaned as she humped her
hips and locked Daniella onto her body, not wanting any
change to this delicious sensation . . . this girl really had it,
whatever it was. I want her for always and always, Sam
promised herself.

'Do you like it?' Daniella asked huskily, raising herself up.
'Do you really?'and Sam saw to her surprise that Daniella
was using both hands to lift herself up but that lovely feeling
was still there inside her.

'Yes . . .' moaned Sam, breathing deeply as Daniella thrust slowly into her virgin vagina. 'Don't stop . . . oh don't stop . . . but . . . what are you doing?'

Daniella giggled. 'I'm in you!' she said. 'It feels so-oo nice, so wonderful, so sweet. . . . I love you Sam. I want you . . . I have never been inside a woman before and . . . oh God . . . I can't help it!'

'AAARRRRhhhh!' Daniella cried out piercingly, almost screaming, and thrust deeply into Sam. Sam cried out too at the deep exquisite stab of pleasure she felt. Then Daniella collapsed onto Sam and lay there, panting. Dripping sweat and make-up. They lay and giggled together like naughty schoolgirls, kissing and joking about the newness of sex with the opposite sex.

Then Daniella got up, put on her filmy negligee and found two champagne glasses and a chilled bottle. Sam clinked her filmed crystal glass against Daniella's and reflected that she could forgo beer for champagne on this unique occasion. She still couldn't believe it. That a *boy* could look like this?

'Here's to *US!*' trilled Daniella.

'To us,' echoed Sam, deeply moved. 'How old are you Daniella?' she asked after watching Daniella pirouette around the room showing off her loveliest clothes.

'Twenty,' giggled Daniella, already on her second glass of

champers, twirling around the room with her gown flying out like Ginger Rogers without Fred Astaire.

'How long have you been dressing like a woman?'

'The last five years, since I left home and got a job.' Daniella opened the double wardrobe which filled one end of the room. It was packed with women's clothes, all a perfect size 10. Underneath, matching shoes were piled in colourful abandon.

Only at one end was there a collection of duller, dark-coloured clothes. Men's clothes, Sam realised. From that end Daniella selected a deep red robe and offered it to Sam.

'Here,' she said. 'Try this on. It's an antique silk dressing gown. It will suit you.' Wearing the robe Sam realised that she looked and felt really masculine and that Daniella, for all the discrepancy in her genitals, was a woman through and through. Far more so than Sam had ever been. Tiddly, they swayed in front of the mirror. Giggling and hugging, looking at themselves. Sam burst out laughing.

'Yeah,' she said, thrusting out her chest and flexing her biceps. 'This dressing gown is me. Look at us! We look just like a heterosexual couple!' she exclaimed.

'Yes,' agreed Daniella, 'I'm the girl and YOU are the boy!' They laughed and laughed until they collapsed on the floor where they began making love all over again.

It was only much later, when she had had time to reflect,

that Sam realised, too late, that Daniella had actually come inside her. Put fresh sperm in her virgin cunt. After thirty barren years.

A male had given her pleasure and it hadn't been at all what she had expected. The other dykes she knew who had tried fucking men all had horror stories about how much it hurt, how revolting and intrusive het sex was. With Daniella none of that was relevant and Sam was unready for what having a male lover implied.

At noon on Sunday Sam reluctantly brought herself to phone home and tell Tiffany where she was. The phone rang four times and the call minder picked it up. Sam hesitated, said 'Tiffany — I'm OK. Just taking some time out. See you on Tuesday.'

Breathing a sigh of relief she turned her cellphone off and put it down on the dressing table beside Daniella's cosmetics. Then she wondered . . . where *is* Tiffany now?

She first noticed him when she was jogging down her street. 'Another bloody old hippie!' she thought, seeing his drab khaki shirt, scruffy jeans, bare feet, his long hair in an untidy knot and a streaked beard down his chest. She put him out of her mind. Not the sort of man I would ever look at. Nah. Not me babe! She jogged through her front gate and unlocked the door. Bounced into the bathroom and stripped off her sweaty tights and T-shirt, dumped her socks and trainers outside the door and almost fell into the cool delight of the shower.

How she loved to have a shower! Those sleek spurts of water massaging her skin! So much better than a bath. God! It was always wonderful. Even after a stressful day dealing with those stroppy rich bastards whom Tiffany's preferred to promote — even then a shower could ease all that tightness in her body.

Fiona turned and turned, now running the hot water on her shoulders, now opening her mouth and greedily drinking the spray, feeling the sweat and tensions of the day wash away. She felt the heat of the run easing in her muscles and she began to feel sensual, to imagine someone was watching her.

She vaguely visualised someone standing there in the bathroom; someone loved, who loved her, who loved to watch her wash herself and then, when she had finished, he would fuck her like a demon on fire . . . Yes. It was for him she was washing now.

Running the soap down the side of her breast, watching the bubbles collect around her nipple and drip off . . . ooze the soap down her breast, slip it into her underarm and massage bubbles into the sweet dark hairs there, her uplifted arm languid, sensual, swaying. She thought of the princess in *Swan Lake* and swung around humming, made a pirouette on one leg, slid almost out of control into the chilly plastic wall. Tossed the soap to her other hand and swooped it down her other arm to massage the armpit then shyly slid it down to her plump round stomach where she drew patterns in the soapiness, slipped her finger into her navel, out again. A swoop down to the top of her pubic hair, long and sleek and curly, where the water dripped in a hundred different drops from the hairs modestly covering her nether lips . . . she played on her stomach and breasts, drawing soapy patterns and then wove them around onto her buttocks which she pointed at her imaginary lover like the heart of gold at the end of the rainbow.

The soap had a lust of its own and her fingers did too. They soaped her sweet rosebud asshole and slid inside, one finger, then two. Her pussy throbbed and she thought of her mystery lover leaning over, inspecting her bottom for cleanliness. Then she slipped her soapy hands between her legs and soaped her hair, her lips, but refrained from entering inside. She never used soap there. It never needed soaping, just a rinse and oh! Rinsing there! She would put that off a little, tease him. Tease herself.

Now she took the showerhead from its holder and played the water over her bottom then tucked herself in and thrust out her breasts, swished the soapiness from them, squeezed them together with the nipples twin cannons at the devil. Ran the water over the top of her head, foaming through her scalp so her hair mermaided over her face.

Peering through the water she grinned at herself in the mirror across the room, flicked her hair aside and crouched down, legs wide, and played the water over her open pussy, the pink silky flesh becoming even pinker as the warm water drummed and drummed at her lips and the tightly budded clit flowered, unfurled and set sail on the oceans of pleasure emanating from the water.

She saw him now, looking closely, watching as her body drew nearer, ever nearer to orgasm and then, she knew, just as she was about to come, he would join her in the shower, lift her up and impale her throbbing, willing body on his enormous cock.

'Ahhhhhhhhhh!' With a loud breathy pulsing cry she came. Suddenly really relaxed, she slumped against the side of the shower. The water was still thrusting endlessly from the showerhead onto the tiles beside her. She shuddered and took several deep breaths before she stood and turned the water off. A few moments later, as she was drying herself off, she heard a knock on the door. Hurriedly she put on the old blue terry-towelling dressing gown her mother gave her when she left home and went to the door.

That weird hippie guy was there! Hadn't she just seen him heading the other way, down towards town?

'Yes?' she said, disagreeably. She folded her arms and frowned at him.

'For you,' he said simply, holding a beautiful bunch of flowers towards her. She was stunned.

'What are they for?' she asked, trying and succeeding not to look as wildly surprised as she really was.

'For you, because you are beautiful,' he said simply. 'Goodnight.' He placed the flowers on her folded arms and walked off up the path to the street. Fiona took the flowers into the bathroom and looked into the mirror at the face she had always known as plain and held the flowers up beside her cheek . . . 'Beautiful! Huh! Tiffany's beautiful, Claudia Schiffer is beautiful. I'm just ordinary,' she said to herself, dropping the flowers on the floor and beginning to get ready for bed.

It was only as Fiona was climbing into bed that she realised he had picked some flowers from every suburban garden between the spot she had seen him and her home. 'Weird bastard,' she said to herself and double locked the doors. Pam, her flatmate, would just have to knock extra loud and wake her up when she got home. With weirdos like that around she wasn't taking any chances.

Next day work was doubly stressful. It was obvious that Sam wasn't coming in to work. She had left a message on the answerphone. She had said, in a strange voice, that she wanted to take sick leave for a week and would they please look after the Art Gallery people with gold-dust-painted cottonwool hands till she got back. Tiffany was looking strained and as if she hadn't had much sleep.

She wouldn't talk about it, even though Fiona asked. Louise and Tiffany were unusually quiet and would look significantly at each other every now and then.

Something's going on, she thought. Wonder what?

Bet, her best friend, was preoccupied. She was going to see her old boyfriend Allen in a few days and she was clearly scatty about it. Not a good idea, thought Fiona, but who am I to know?

So she felt like the only normal one in their usually talkative group. She ended up fielding some very difficult calls from the gallery people and they were not pleased at all to hear that their Sam was away on leave. They all wanted to know why and Fiona didn't know the reason.

All in all, it was a frustrating day.

She saw the hippie again that evening as she was jogging. He had on the same old jeans but a checked shirt and jandals tonight. His hair was an awful mess. She thought about burying her face in that hairy mess and nearly threw up on the pavement.

Geez — I hope I don't see him again. I suppose he lives

87

around here somewhere. Spare me from neighbours like that!

Pam was home and answered the door. Fiona was in the shower and Pam poked her head into the bathroom and said, 'Some hippie left you a bunch of flowers. He left a message too. On a card. Do you want me to read it to you?'

'Yeah — OK,' called Fiona, wondering, worrying now. What could this dude want? Pam laughed and said, 'It says — to the most beautiful woman in the world.' She giggled. 'Nice flowers though. They look like the ones you got for us last night.' Fiona frowned and said, 'That silly bugger brought me those too. Would you believe it! What is he up to, I wonder?'

'Wants to get into your pants if you ask me,' said Pam. 'I'll put them in some water shall I? I think you used our only vase last night.'

After another difficult day Fiona went jogging again and tried a different route. She passed the hippie walking up some narrow steps as she was running down them.

'Good evening,' he said softly as she tried to slip invisibly by him.

She said 'Hi' and ran, her body tingling as she felt him watching her as she raced away from him towards home. When she looked in the letterbox there was a small wrapped gift. 'To the loveliest woman in the world,' said the card. Her hands shook as she took it inside and she felt deliciously excited as she opened it. Inside was a tiny hand-carved bone filigree heart in a tissue nest.

'Look at this!' she said in amazement to Pam. 'What an amazing little thing. Do you think he made it?'

'Dunno,' said Pam, 'but it kind of looks unique. I've never seen anything like that before.'

'The tissue has a lovely perfume on it too . . .' said Fiona. 'Maybe he isn't such a hippie after all. Who is he?' she wondered. 'What is he up to?'

The following evenings Fiona jogged again but she didn't see the hairy hippie at all. Gradually she flopped into a lonely depression. Work was shit and she looked forward to the possibility of gifts from a strange man and now — nothing.

Disappointment. She talked sternly to herself. He means nothing. He's mad anyway. Why would he give a stranger gifts? He's an awful type of man, sloppy, probably smelly, no money or job, probably lives in the park at the top of the hill. Had millions of women while he lived in a commune, for all I know. Yuk. But she thought about him at work and at home and she in her turn became absent-minded.

A taxi drew up outside the front gate. The driver honked and then came in.

'I have been instructed to pick up the most beautiful woman in the world and take her to a mystery destination!' he announced, grinning, thoroughly enjoying his job for once.

Fiona freaked out.

'Pam, help me please! It's HIM again! Should I go or not! Is it safe? Who IS it?' She stood in the hallway panicking.

The taxi driver grinned all the more and said, 'Come on, luv. I'm instructed to take you to a certain public place. If you want to leave, once you get there, there are plenty of taxis available. OK?'

'Go on! Just go Fiona. What have you got to lose? I wish it was me,' said Pam enviously. So Fiona went. After all, she thought, this kind of thing doesn't happen every day. I'd be consumed with curiosity for the rest of my life if I didn't go and Tiffany would tell me to go, I just know she would. Fiona quickly threw on her jeans, jacket and boots. She felt more self-possessed in them than her work clothes.

The taxi had yet another bunch of flowers in it and the driver dropped her off outside one of the most expensive restaurants in the garden belt of town and left her. No one seemed to be waiting.

She felt really silly, standing there on the street in a leather jacket holding a big bunch of stolen flowers. She looked around, couldn't see him anywhere and sighed. Silly bloody wild goose chase, she thought. Looked at her watch.

I will wait here for ten minutes and if something doesn't happen I will just get a taxi home again.

She leaned up against the fence of the restaurant's garden bar. The minutes ticked by with elephantine slowness. From inside the restaurant came sounds of laughter and happy eating; fairy music seemed to surround her in the soft evening air.

'Good evening,' said a soft, cultured voice behind her. Fiona jumped and quickly moved away from the fence. He was there, on the other side of the fence and dimly she saw that there were tables and chairs there too, almost invisible in the darkness.

'Shit! You gave me a fright!' she exclaimed. He smiled, teeth gleaming white from within his beard.

'Welcome to our first evening out,' he said calmly, standing up, gesturing in a courtly way for her to enter the gate and join him. When she was opposite him he said, 'Jim Morrison, at your service.' And held out his hand. He looked and sounded like one of the dwarves from *The Hobbit*. Fiona laughed.

'Fiona,' she said and shook his hand firmly. He gripped hers with equal strength and she was stunned by the bolt of electricity which shot from his hand into her body.

'I think you haven't had dinner yet,' he said. 'Would you please have dinner with me?'

'Well I'm here now!' Fiona laughed again. 'I might as well.' She sat down, tried to relax, looked more closely at him. He lit the three candles on their table, their only illumination, and called the waiter over.

'Red or white?' he asked her.

'Uh – red,' she said, not ready for anything, swimming far from the shore deep in the pond of bewilderment. He looked different. His hair was combed and bound back elegantly. His beard, too, had a few grey streaks in it, but seemed clean, cleaner than she would have thought. She could smell a subtle cologne. His body was clean and tonight he was wearing a white cotton pleated pirate shirt with a waistcoat and some kind of dark pants – maybe even shoes or they wouldn't have let him in this place. Damn it – he even looked handsome.

When the waiter had gone he leaned over and took her hand. 'I apologise if I have embarrassed you. But I have fallen in love with you and this was the only way I could think of to get you interested in me.' His voice was soft and all sincerity.

Fiona opened her eyes wide. 'The message did get through,' she said, 'about love, from you. But you don't know me! You know nothing about me!' she exclaimed. 'You're nuts! Really truly crazy!'

'Am I?' Jim asked, leaning back, relaxed, self-assured. He smiled at her and she felt a thrill of delight run through her.

'If you really think I am crazy, what are you doing out at dinner with a madman?' He raised his eyebrows and suddenly she saw him not as a hippie but as an educated, magnetic personality and she began to wonder just who he was, what he did, where he lived. Suddenly he leaned forward and took her hand, although how he found it Fiona didn't know. He just seemed to have some attraction for her hand and it was his without her permission.

'Sweet Fiona . . . if that is really your name. I have watched you for weeks and adored you from a distance until I could bear it no longer.' She shivered as chills ran through her . . . a voyeur, a man who watches . . . yes! He lifted her hand to his lips and they burned through her skin, heating her body through and through. She laughed and pulled her hand away.

'I've never had anyone kiss my hand before,' she said. 'I'm not used to it.' The wine arrived and they drank, eyes boring into each other, wary, wondering, wanting and rejecting all at once.

They talked, sparred, all through dinner and he did not touch her again. She worried about herself. Perversely, now he wasn't touching her, she wanted his touch. Bloody women! Always wanting what isn't there. What we shouldn't have.

Jim was powerful, mysterious and intelligent. He said he

93

worked for a US company as a consultant part-time and spent the rest of his time writing poetry and lecturing at the university. He seemed at once romantic, exotic. He had grown up in Argentina and Hamilton. And suddenly there was no penniless hippie for her to see and she could not remember the hairy man who picked flowers in her street. She now saw a strong intelligent employed man who chose to look like whatever he felt like that day and she was falling like a stone into a limpid pool of desire.

After liqueur, she felt aroused, desired him. She would in fact have desired anyone but she was too proud to admit that and when he called a cab her heart sank. 'Goodbye my goddess,' he said and kissed her burning hand again before she got into the taxi. He didn't even say when I would see him again, she thought despairingly as the car sped her homeward.

'Well? How did it go?' asked Pam keenly when Fiona walked in the door.

Fiona laughed and leaned against the wall. She was reeling, dazed, drunk, though she had only had two glasses of wine and a liqueur. Now she was at home she knew she was really gone on Jim. Gone, how embarrassing! In love after a dinner and his lips on her hand twice. Shit! How could she tell Pam that? She'd never felt like this about anyone even after sleeping with them.

'Aw — it was OK,' she said.

'Just OK?' asked Pam. 'You look like it was more than a bit of OK to me,' she commented sleazily, raising her eyebrows at Fiona. Fiona blushed.

'Absolutely nothing happened,' she said defensively. 'Nothing! Believe me! There is nothing in it. Jim says he loves me but he's too old for me. He has that huge hairy awful beard too. Urgh! I could never fuck a man like that!' But in bed she dreamed of him, saw his smile, imagined him watching her while she showered and knew he would. Oh yes. He will do anything for you. Plain old you, Fiona. Believe him, he wants you very much.

There is nothing so arousing as being wanted. Fiona was aroused and tossed and turned, not wanting to come thinking of him, but near dawn her hands were busy squeezing and teasing her nipples, her fingers dipping and rolling and massaging her pussy and she came, long and shuddering, drowning in the sweet sensation of Jim and his love, the surety of his lust.

After two days of silence from Jim she was frantic. She couldn't even work. Fiona could pay no attention to anything for more than five minutes. Tiffany's seemed to be falling apart. Sam had come back but wouldn't talk about why she went away. She had moved out of her apartment with Tiffany and was living with someone else. She wouldn't talk about who or introduce her to them. Tiffany seemed devastated and guilty simultaneously. Fiona didn't understand it, but Louise was implicated somewhere although Sam seemed happy. Strange if Louise and Tiffany were getting it on! But *are* they? And Bet! Shit, Bet was impossible. She would talk of nothing but Allen morning, noon and night till you wished the whole National Party would just get on and drown in the sea! She hadn't done more than talk to him for a couple of minutes on the phone but that was enough.

Fiona jogged faithfully every night after work and Jim wasn't there. The letterbox was empty. No taxis arrived and the phone didn't ring even though he now knew her number. She felt so wild with him she wanted to scream, beat him up, cry, beg him to call. It was the most hateful, wonderful way to feel, so intoxicated by someone you desperately wanted to see. Someone who, a week ago, was nothing to you.

She saw him watching her as she showered every night and she came strong and hard thinking of him in her. His strong fat cock thrusting, thrusting and God! How she wanted him.

Finally she cried, late at night, wetting her pillow and giving him up for lost. She let him go. Tossed him out into the deep green void of oblivion and vowed to forget him. God. It is only a week and a half since I first saw him on the street. He probably has a wife and kids at home. You're a fool Fiona, she said to herself. Just a damn fool. She chucked the flowers out onto the compost pile and put the tiny locket away in her undies drawer at the back.

♋

Everyone at the office went out for dinner at the Istanbul, their favourite restaurant, and talked about the future of Tiffany's. It was very difficult and uncomfortable. But they had always been honest with each other about where they were going and what they were doing. Tiffany was subdued and just sat quietly, asking each one of them in turn what they wanted for the future and if they were willing to continue working at Tiffany's for the next six months. Louise sat beside Tiffany and held her hand. She said she would support Tiffany in whatever she wanted for the agency.

Sam was quiet but said that she could see no reason why she should not stay until the end of the Art Gallery contract if Tiffany had no objections. Tiffany burst into tears but finally admitted she had no problem with that. Sam wouldn't answer questions about her new girlfriend at all. She just smiled and fiddled with her earrings. 'You'll find out soon enough,' was all she said.

Bet was content with things as they were. She was impatient to see Allen though and if anyone had shown the slightest interest would have warbled on and on about her preparations to see him and what she imagined would happen.

Fiona couldn't say anything except that her life was normal. Well – kind of normal. What can you say about a man who appears in your life one week and is gone the next? Of course she wanted to stay working for Tiffany's. They were all founder members and it was now very successful. Who had a choice? Nothing else would pay as well.

Fiona came home exhausted. 'Bloody women! These lesbians are impossible! But I can't complain. At least I still have my job!' she muttered to herself as she walked up the garden path to the front door. She sighed after looking in the empty letterbox and walked inside to find the house full of flowers. Dozens of orchid sprays wrapped in sparkling cellophane had arrived after work. Pam had received them and distributed them around the house in one-litre plastic milk bottles, the only suitable containers they had.

'He surely believes in flowers!' laughed Pam.

Fiona sat on the floor and laughed too. Then she cried

and looked at each spike of exquisitely shaded and coloured blooms and found no note. Nothing.

'I HATE you, Jim!' she shouted to thin air then went to bed and cried herself to sleep.

She looked his name up in the University Calendar and phoned him at his office. He wasn't in. She almost had a tantrum in frustration. She asked the departmental secretary for his home number, said she was a student of his and got it. She sat looking at it in triumph. Ha! Two can play this game! She phoned it and got his voice on the answerphone. Froze, couldn't leave a message and put the phone down. God, I need some Valium. What am I doing? Why am I wasting my time?

And she sat, numbly looking out at the lights of the city, lost in the wildness of her feelings, of what all these apparently adoring gifts had done to her. Remembering the touch of Jim's hand, the elegant, faintly foreign way he spoke.

The phone rang and she jumped out of her skin in fright. Trembling she picked it up.

'Goddess,' he said. 'Sweet Fiona, I apologise for my lack of contact but there was a crisis with the company and I had to step in and clean the mess up.' As he spoke she melted into mush. 'May I see you tomorrow night? You aren't busy on a Friday night? There isn't another man you'd rather be with?'

Trembling, she laughed. 'No. You know I don't have a man in my life at the moment. I'd love to spend some time with you.'

'Good. I will come for you at about seven. Is that OK?'

'Yes,' she said softly. 'And thank you for the flowers.'

'The pleasure is all mine. Sweet dreams until we meet again.'

She almost contemplated taking Friday off so she could catch up on her sleep, do her make-up properly, get out and buy a new dress. Find some wonderful perfume. But she steeled herself and reported in. The Art Gallery were more amenable today. Sam was sorting them out. She had closed the contract anyway and they all put their heads together brainstorming ideas, their best skill, to begin developing the finer points of the new campaign.

All through the day she was impatient, longing, tingling, wanting to be with Jim. Fantasising about him, how he would be as a lover. Almost every hour she would find a strong vision growing from her gut, squeezing out reality. Jim, strong and naked. His penis thick and fat and somehow extremely masculine despite the fact it wasn't huge or long. Jim holding his cock and stroking it, pumping it, looking at her as she pirouetted in front of him dressed in a diaphanous gown and shawl which she swirled about her, hiding now her nipples, now her hips, then her lips, teasing, always teasing and getting closer and closer to him as he watched, hungrily drinking her in. Focused on her as no other man had been before. Plain Fiona desired, loved.

Of course she would get interrupted before she got further into the fantasy but the tension grew and grew in her long-neglected body. Her sex was wet and wetter. By mid-afternoon she had to wear a pantyshield. She blushed as she tried to stick it to her soaking panties. She felt ashamed of wanting him, of desiring sex so very much. When she stood in front of the mirror and straightened her dress, she saw a different woman, bright-eyed, flushed cheeks, aroused and expectant. The nearest she could get to this feeling from her past was the night the netball team had stayed overnight in the school hall. She had been fourteen years old. She giggled. What a bloody boring life I have had! 'Till now . . .' she whispered. 'Till now . . .!'

She decided not to tell the others just yet. Let Jim be her secret. Just for a while. Until she knew if they — if she . . . just wait.

She didn't go jogging that evening; she showered instead and in place of the mysterious stranger it was Jim watching her as the sweet hot jets of water pummelled her clit to orgasm. She couldn't help it, a few seconds and she was thrust over the top, drowning in pleasure and moaning with the flannel shoved in her mouth because Pam was at home and she didn't dare cry out in the shower. If Pam had sex with the shower she didn't let on and Fiona wasn't going to either.

She looked again and again at her three favourite dresses. She didn't like any of them. They were too conservative, too boring to wear for Jim. She wanted a fabulous dress! A dress of wild red lace with a gauzy silky lining, cut low over her small but perfect breasts which she could squeeze, just, into a wonderbra and then she'd have a cleavage, well, a small one. She'd love to show him a cleavage. She longed to shower for him. With him.

She sighed and selected the black velvet sheath. Boring but OK. Kind of sophisticated. No frills and no lace. He could see what he was getting.

She had just put on her lipstick when there was a knock on the door. Pam answered it before Fiona could open her bedroom door. 'It's Mr Morrison, for you!' she trilled in triumph. Fiona was happy to allow Pam her little treats. 'Out in a minute!' she called back and heard Pam showing him into the tiny lounge.

Her hands shook and she took a good ten minutes composing herself, making her whole body calm down. She lay on the bed, put her feet up the wall, thought of fixing the leak in the toilet cistern and work on Monday. The whole vertiginous space of the weekend, full of potentially divine prospects, yawned before her. She swung her legs to the floor and put her high heels on. 'Sorry I'm so slow,' she said, smiling at him as she glided into the living room.

'Oh! You look divine!' exclaimed Pam. Jim grinned as he got up out of their most tatty armchair. 'Divine indeed!' he said as he took her hands and kissed one. He led the way and on the street outside was his car, a metallic gold Mercedes with an electric top. He still looked like a hippie, she decided. It was just that in the setting of the leather seats of his car, with the sunlight of a spring evening shining on him, he was very different to the man she had seen at first, with his stolen bunch of flowers.

Jim's long hair and beard showed gold, grey, red and black. He had combed and perfumed it and suddenly she saw in him a herd of multicoloured horses, galloping this way and that; virile, wild and very sexy.

She sat back in the seat of his car and laughed. Freedom! Now she could relax and enjoy the evening and whatever would come. She wriggled as she felt the freedom of no panties and the constriction of the wonderbra on her normally unrestrained breasts.

Jim drove fast and wild up the winding narrow road to the lookout over the city and harbour. He got out and walked over to the wall bounding the edge of the view. He sat down and watched her walk towards him, swaying in her high heels. He smiled and she smiled back. How silly, how inane, she thought, look at us two. As she stood close to him, looking out at the magnificent sunny view, pretending not to notice him, secretly smiling at how cool, how utterly cool she almost felt, he leaned forward and put his arms around her, placed his head on her belly and hugged her body to him. She found herself stroking his hair and swaying with him. After a few moments he sat back and pulled her onto his lap.

Fiona lay back against Jim's shoulder and smiled at him. Words were unnecessary between them. She felt like Cinderella Barbie stepping out of the pumpkin coach in her new dress with the Prince at her feet.

Jim began to trace her lips and eyes and hairline with his fingers, brushed his hand over her face and then, ever so slowly, brought his lips to meet hers. She smelt his breath, the odour of his skin and hair, felt the tickle of his beard and moustache and then . . . the sweet warm touch of his mouth as he massaged her lips with his. Not caring she was wearing lipstick he slowly teased her lips, easing her mouth open, running his tongue along her lips, nibbling her upper lip and then her lower lip. Then he sealed her mouth for a moment with his, and — ah! He pulled away from her.

'Wow!' Fiona whispered and looked at him, eyes wide. 'I've never been kissed like that before.'

Jim's arms tightened around her. 'I haven't either,' he said softly and brushed her forehead with his lips again. She was enveloped in his beard for a moment and she found it warm, sweet, softer than she had imagined. Fiona lay in his arms and stared out over the city. The day seemed full of melted gold, like some wild hyper-real soft drink advertisement and she took a deep breath in, shuddered, let it out and her body flowed into Jim and he into her. After what could have been a long time he said, 'Dinner? Do you think?' Fiona laughed and shook herself out of the comfort zone of him. 'Yes! We were supposed to have dinner — let's.'

As they dined Jim often took her hand, touched her thigh, or her arm. She grew braver and would reach out to touch his hand, lift his fingers to her lips, run the sharp edges of her teeth along the sides of his fingers. He would hiss in delight and brighten like a flame. She loved his responses. She'd been out with so many men who wouldn't respond at all either in public or private to anything she did and now there was Jim.

Here, alive, connected to his skin, sensual and loving. She had the feeling he would appreciate anything she did and, safe in the comfort of his acceptance, she bloomed. She snuggled into him and stroked his beard as they talked softly, watching the candles gutter down into their stubs.

Again the Mercedes took them into the hills, climbed up to his flat high on the most expensive hillside, overlooking the gut-wrenching wide swoop of the night-lit harbour. The city hills reflected above like phosphorescence transferred to air. Liquid gold, mercury and pearl on the water lapping the shores far below.

As Fiona stood on the balcony Jim was close behind her and stroked her shoulders. He put his arms around her waist and murmured about how long he had waited for this night. She laughed a long low giggle — no man had ever seemed so loving, so sincere and she could hardly believe it.

Jim crouched behind her and lifted her dress up. In one swoop he whipped it off over her head and she was naked except for the wonderbra. He slowly unclasped that and let her pert breasts free. She stood, limned in the light from the night city, naked and vulnerable and open to him. She danced naked around the balcony as he watched, delighted at her vivacity, and then laid her body against his big chest.

'Oh Jim!' Fiona said softly. 'My God, Jim.' Because she knew she would never know what he was going to do next. Never. He walked around and around her, drinking in her nakedness and then stood in front of her and said, 'Your turn.' She slowly undressed him. Taking her time, the wind chilling her a little, her nipples standing out as she unbuttoned his silk shirt. It flew away into a corner and uncovered his big barrel chest, hairy and warm as toast. Then his black leather pants, unbuckle, slide them down, shuck off his shoes and his briefs remained, pressed out tautly by his erection. Kneeling in front of him she gently lifted the elastic band up and over his cock and laid her cheek on his hot erection as she slid the briefs to his ankles. She held them down as he stepped out of them and hugged him to her.

Smelling the sex aroma of his body she cradled his balls in her hands, rubbed her face over and over his cock as it dripped onto her face and she licked up the slick juice. Fiona felt her body move, bond with him, marry with Jim as the taste of his desire dissolved on her tongue. She moaned and began licking and licking his sex. Stroking her nipples up and down his thighs, cupping her breasts under his testicles, every few moments engulfing his cock with her hungry mouth. Eager for that gorgeous taste to invade her again. Ooooooo. So very, very hungry, needy for him. Waiting for him and now found. Completion, joy . . .

He twined his hands in her silky hair, swooping his hands over her scalp in a firm massaging stroke. The same rhythm as that which she used to suck him. Tight and tighter he pulled her hair until he said loudly, 'Stop! Stop!' and then softer, 'Ahhhhh.' He lifted her up and cradled her body against his.

Beyond all was light, gold, silver, neon and chill of wind, and between them heat that seemed to melt into her marrow. She breathed deeply and kissed him, drinking him in, slipping her hands into his long full hanks of hair, unfastening it, allowing it to be as free as their bodies and hearts. His hair covered his shoulders and his beard his big chest, and now, somehow, she treasured this abundance. It covered an inner abundance and did not hide but advertised something special.

Jim set her down, moved her thighs apart with his and pressed his hand up against her mons. Fiona moaned, leaned back and allowed herself to relax into him as his fingers bewitched her further, delving into her, sliding out, teasing, stroking her clit lightly, slick with her desire for him. Her vagina aching hard for his penis which pressed insistently between them, into her belly, promising pleasure, fulfilment and ecstasy if only it were inside in this position instead of outside.

Jim ignored his penis and stroked and stroked Fiona until she began moaning rhythmically and almost fainted from pleasure into his arms. He lifted her body and carried her into his bedroom, laid her on his big bed and lit a candle. He pulled her towards him until her bottom was at the edge and parted her legs. Impulsively he kissed her wet lips and then held the candle close as he parted her outer lips and gazed at her throbbing desiring crying cunt. Her clit was fully out of hiding and a continuous slickness lubricated her and dripped slowly out of her.

With his index finger Jim traced her inner lips, stroked her clit so gently she shuddered and cried out . . . 'Ahhhhh!' Fiona wanted to shout, 'Jim! Fuck me now!' She wanted to kneel in front of him, beg him to impale her now on that gorgeous cock but she knew, somehow, that he would do exactly as he pleased and impulsive lust was not what tonight was about.

Parting her cunt lips wide he pressed his mouth to her vagina and drank deeply of her. She gazed unseeing at the ceiling, lights flashing in front of her eyes then stars exploding as he sucked on her clit. She screamed. She didn't hear herself but her throat became hoarse from unaccustomed use. Placing the candle aside Jim commenced to play her most intimate soft wet parts as if they were a complicated instrument of ecstasy. Licking, touching, blowing cool breath, hot touches, pinches and tiny bites, blowing bubbles onto her clit. Sliding never more than one finger into her, tormenting her and taking Fiona over and over again to the brink of ecstasy.

Then, knowing and growing in knowing, he would change

what he was doing and she would find herself further and further away from orgasm but with a crescendo building inside her body like an immense tidal wave. He rose up from between her legs just as she was desperate, writhing, begging, babbling, hyperventilating, an open flower needing, wanting, and he grasped her breasts. Leaned his head down and pressed his penis against her slick cuntlips.

She clasped her legs around him ecstatically and tried to slip him inside her. He would not allow it. Kept his penis immovable, how did he do that? Just pressed and pressed against her open wet lips and clit and lowered his head and softly bit her nipples. The electric sensations zapped her most intimate parts deep inside and she cried, tears running down her cheeks. After an eternity of suspense he moved up from her nipples and pressed his mouth covered in her juices to her lips. She surrendered to the taste of the two of them on their lips, melding and mixing.

Suddenly his penis slid deep within her and she went rigid, her cry of ecstasy buried in Jim's enveloping mouth. Slowly he began to thrust into her and with each thrust she died in a stroke of lightning and then lived to drown again. Wave after wave crashed over her and still on and on he thrust, lifting her hips up off the bed he stood and looked at her lovely body, at her ecstasy, revelling in her cries of pleasure as he thrust. Then he pulled out and sucked her clit until the very finest edge of orgasm and again thrust into her. Picking her up off the bed, her legs and arms clasped around him as she came at last, her vagina gripping and gripping him as she sobbed and sobbed. Her tears wet his hair and beard as he allowed himself to meld with her for the first time. Thrusting three more times he allowed the dam to release itself. His seed burst into her with a great cry mingling with her cries. Firmly Fiona held onto him with her arms and legs as, trembling with release, he lowered them down onto the bed at last.

Shuddering for a long time they lay as one. Softly murmuring, kissing and laughing. Crying . . . Fiona wept because in all her twenty-nine years she had never had sex like this, like Jim. After such joy what was left? Could they ever repeat it? Could they? Jim assured her they could and would.

'Are you fertile?' he asked her.

'Uh – yes,' she said, suddenly conscience-stricken, panic gripping her belly. Fiona hadn't had a lover in so long that she had forgotten she wasn't on the pill and she had assumed that he would use a condom. He hadn't, as it turned out, but Jim had known or guessed she wasn't on the pill.

'Very soon you will be pregnant with a child – our child – a love child.'

Fiona freaked out.

'My God! What a stupid bitch I am!' she wailed. He calmed her down.

'There is nothing to worry about – please, beautiful Fiona – please marry me. Bear our child. Be my wife. Let's share life together?' His asking was of the most persuasive kind, his penis throbbing and erect within her again.

What have I got to lose? As he kissed her and slowly slid in and out of her body again, planting his seed deeper within her, she knew the bliss of absolute trust for the first time and she whispered, 'Yes . . . I will marry you, Jim Morrison. I want you more than I have ever wanted anyone. I care about you and it is time I had a child.'

He leaned over her, his eyes a blaze of happiness, laid his head on her belly and wept with big sobs of release and joy.

Fiona never wondered why.

8

$\mathcal{B}$et was wringing her serviette into shreds as she waited for Allen at Café Victoria beside the harbour. She had always loved the sea. It sloshed up against the sea wall beside her, reflecting the sun in shards of blinding light off the high-rise buildings and the wicker tables and chairs of the café. While Bet waited her thoughts arrived in wild anxious spurts.

Hey Allen, she thought to him, rehearsing what she could say. It's weird how things happen, how life has happened to us. Here we are with the salt spray and sea breeze too. It's making a mess of my hair but shit man! Here we are again. I never thought this would happen — did you? I remember us so clearly. All those useless, faceless men I've sampled over the last ten years were like water to me, compared to the melted-wax heat of your mouth on mine. Once we were side by side, life and death and serious fucking. I thought our love would never end, that we'd marry, have those kids you've got from someone else.

Ahhhh . . . you sucking my fingers, your cock hard inside your jeans. My cunt wet and wanting your mouth and moustache pressed deep and hard. I am sure you won't feel like that today. Bet sighed and shredded more pink paper into the sea breeze.

Beside her on the pier a child caught a spotty and as she watched the father drew up the laden fishing line, the helpless suffocating fish flipping, swinging, skittering in a frantic effort to escape an alien atmosphere. His hand closing firmly around it, spiked fins wet and cold, hook taken out clean then an unclean sharp knife cutting suddenly through spine and backbone onto the rough tarred black concrete.

Bet shuddered, remembering herself like a female fish, hooked on Allen and then the sharp razor slice of his voice, never forgotten, over the phone . . . 'Sorry, Bet,' he had said. 'Sorry.' Would sorry ever make anything better, heal that

dead fish or my dead heart? It was no wonder she'd felt like
– tried to. Never mind – that won't happen again. No Bet, she
told herself firmly. It won't happen again.

As she watched the fish being cut into bait-sized chunks,
bloody on the tarry wall, a warm familiar male voice said,
'Gidday!' cheerfully, and she stood, knocking over her chair
as Allen, breezy and self-assured in a dark-blue suit with a
bright red tie came striding towards her. He was plumper
now, not as fit as when he played rugby, Bet thought. But her
heart fluttered like that fish on the barbed hook as he
grabbed her hand and shook it.

'Hello Allen,' she said, all her rehearsal flying out the
window, emotions flooding over her in a rising tide. Tears
came to her eyes, surprising her, and her serviette was gone,
blown away in the wind.

'You're looking well,' he announced as men do, really
saying that she looked sexy and good enough to eat and fuck.
His eyes backed up this message and Bet blushed. Their
bodies were still attuned after all these years despite kids,
elections and lovers. 'I don't have long but we can have
coffee. What can I get you?' Allen had gained some
sophistication in parliament and while his eyes lingered
fractionally on her cleavage, as Bet had guessed they would,
he was circumspect and had acquired a politically correct
Wellington style. He was brisk and yet not off-putting.

Bet smiled at him and said, 'I'll have a white wine thanks.' They were silent a while, enjoying looking at each other, catching up on the changes that time had made. 'I know about your wife,' Bet raised the topic that was foremost in her mind. 'How many kids have you got? Three or is it four?' I'm trying to be sociable here, she thought, do a typical little chat. I really want to scream BE MINE NOW! But I won't. I am too well brought up for that. More fool me. But maybe . . . maybe I can catch my fish . . .

He grinned and rubbed his hands together. 'Four of the little blighters. Yeah.' Grinning wide, proud of himself. 'The boys all play rugby too. They're going to be big bastards. Like me.'

'What about you?' he asked, leaning forward. 'Any kids, hubby?'

'No kids. No boyfriend or husband. Just a wonderful job at Tiffany's, our advertising company.'

Bet stopped, then went on, 'I've been thinking about you — you and me, Allen.' He raised his eyebrows.

'I've always loved only you. Boring isn't it? None of the other men I have met ever matched up to you.' He laughed and moved uncomfortably in his chair. 'I may as well be honest with you. There's no point not being honest, not now.' Bet looked down into her wineglass. She waited for him to reply.

Allen was silent. He turned his chair around to face the harbour. The handlines were anchored in the water again. Patiently waiting for another bite on the sweet sharp hook, on the succulent pieces of fresh fish impaled on the rusting barb. Bet turned her wicker chair the same way too. Away from his face, from the threat of rejection. She stretched out her legs, feigning a relaxation she did not feel.

They sat silently, watching the westering sun gild with gold the gorse on the far hills, Soames Island in the centre of the harbour, the cars zooming home along the motorway. Behind them the city roared at rush hour and sirens hooned wildly into the distance.

Allen turned towards her and asked softly, 'You aren't disgusted with what we used to do?'

Bet smiled at him tenderly. 'No. I remember all the things we did and I loved them. I'd like to make love with you and baby powder and everything again.' With her hands sweating and her heart racing she sat as if glued to the chair, willing him to say yes. Yes please, let's be lovers again.

He sighed deeply. 'My wife doesn't know about that — that her breasts are like mum's. I've never powdered her. Back then I thought if I wanted a political career I'd better have a normal life. So I chose a loyal basic woman, we have lots of kids and a happy home. Even if it isn't all I'd like in a home.' He reached out and took her hand, looked at her fingers, slim and delicate in his big hand, stroked the palm of her hand, sending shudders through her body. He took a deep breath, held it, then sighed again.

'Oh Bet,' his voice was soft. 'I can't offer you anything. I want you very much. More than I ever thought I would and . . . I wish now that I'd married you. That I'd become a stock agent or lawyer or something private. Out of the public eye. I'm only a backbencher in this government and I am just a boy in that mob. I get ordered around by the whips and my movements are watched pretty closely.' Bet tightened her fingers, gripping his hand sympathetically. He looked up suddenly, his eyes blazing into hers.

'Yes!' he hissed. 'Let's do it. Bet – please be my mistress. If you can cope with being alone a lot . . .'

Bet tried to think but the blaze of fiery joy was a tornado inside her and she'd happily trade anything, anything at all for his body beside her again even if it was only one night a week. 'I can cope,' she assured him. 'I want to be with you, spend time with you, even if I am only your mistress.' He still loves me! He still wants me! Her heart sang over and over.

'Oh God,' Allen said intensely, leaning towards her. 'How I long to fuck you while wearing those nappies again, Bet. You have no idea how much I want that. It's stupid isn't it? Such an infantile thing.'

'I often wondered where it came from, the babying,

mothering things we did. I enjoyed them too. The feeling of being totally safe, warm and bathed and powdered. Do we feel sexual when we are babies?' Bet wondered.

'I did research it once,' Allen said, relaxing now, drinking his cold coffee, smiling. 'I suppose my mum kept me in nappies too long. Or maybe I was just an early developer and figured that any contact with my cock was great and having my nappy changed was the beginning of everything greater and better.'

'Well I have missed it and never dared to do it with anyone else,' said Bet.

'Yeah.' Allen was heartfelt. 'Would you collect up everything we will need?'

'Oh yes!' Bet was thrilled.

'Here's my private number at my flat here in Wellington. If I get any sleep that is where I have it. Here's my pager number and my office. You can leave messages there. Will that be OK for you?'

'Uh-huh,' said Bet, looking at the business cards he had given her, one with his address scribbled on the back. 'I really think I should have a nickname — you know, one that no one would suspect? If I am going to leave messages for you. I'd love to say it was your mum calling but I suppose everyone knows your parents are dead so — what about "Aunty Glad"?'

He looked at her, smiling. 'Maybe you should be in

parliament instead of me!' he said jokingly. 'That's good, really good. Aunty Glad it is then. You may have difficulty getting through to me sometimes. E-mail's often the best — here.' He took back one of the cards and scribbled something on it. 'My private e-mail address.'

She was dazed and delighted with him, with her sly intelligence, something she did not know she had. It's deeper into the personal now, she thought. You and me, Allen, not teenage lovers any longer. We are more. We are what was never there before. Lust and fishing, desire in the cool wind, warm sun setting, distant waves crashing on boulder beaches. Age accreting a wrinkled limpet life on our bodies. Now we're committed to each other. Not experimenting. Now we're willing to risk. I'm risking loneliness and you're risking your job, your lifestyle with your wife.

Red and gold the sun sets over Oriental Bay. Your babyblues of fire attracting me. My grey moth wings to the flame, eyes blinded by the pheromones of remembrance.

'Thanks for the numbers,' said Bet. 'Here's my phone number at work, see, there's my home number and I will get Louise to set me up an e-mail address. She's our Internet whizz kid.' Allen slipped the tiny cards into his inner suit pocket. 'I can cope,' Bet said confidently, smiling. 'I will wait for you. No matter how long it takes I'll wait to see you again.'

'It's coming up to Christmas,' Allen said intensely, warning her. 'I may not be able to see you at all until after the House sits again in February.' Bet was blank with shock. So close, so close and the cup of joy dashed from her lips just as she was about to gulp happiness from it.

'When *can* I see you then?' she asked softly, tears spilling out of her eyes without her permission.

Allen pulled out his cellphone, dialled a number and spoke rapidly into it. The machine was ridiculously tiny in his huge hand. Bet wondered how he managed to hit the correct buttons. She began to shiver; the sun had sunk behind the hills and the breeze was chill.

After what seemed like forever Allen clicked the cellphone shut and said, 'How about next Wednesday night? They haven't declared urgency for the House yet. When they do I'll be there from 9 am till 2 am or longer every day until all the legislation the bulldozer wants passed is passed.' He groaned, 'It's hell being an MP. I've never worked harder in my life, really I haven't. So — how about that for a start?' He leaned over towards her, gazing at her breasts lustfully, grabbed both her hands and rubbed them between his.

'God, you're cold!' he exclaimed. Bet smiled, over the moon and gone to heaven.

'Yes! Yes please,' she said softly but intensely, wanting her words to be a blade of certainty that would cut through this political crap to the nub of their love and allow the dross to leave them alone. She wanted the Tardis to suddenly appear in that boring prosaic street of Wellington. So they could run up the street together, open that old blue door and enter the room with no end. Travel to another world bounded by his parents' house in Invercargill. Revisit the park, the steamy bathroom and the big double bed under the uneven slope of the aged bisonboard ceiling.

What am I doing? Allen thought. Ah, lust. It must be lust, that old animal instinct, mixed with power, passion and familiarity. 'What are we doing, Bet?' he asked.

'Shit, Allen? What are we doing? Is this a mistake? I want you so very much and I'm so scared. It is all new now isn't it? We are both different people.'

He laughed and his jumbled teeth flashed at her, rearranged by years of rugby. 'Yeah. I reckon it is new and strange and dangerous. But not so new that I don't want you to go out to Deka and get those special things you know we need.'

Bet sparkled. 'Do you really? I will, I warn you. I'll go and get them . . . a brush, powder, some n – '

'Shush!' he whispered. 'Don't tell me. Surprise me.' He stood up and stretched. Bet saw that his cock was erect inside his suit pants. Allen looked at his watch. 'I better get going. We get paid well but we have to work our asses off to stay there.' He kissed Bet on the cheek and walked away. He hailed a taxi and it roared off. Bet saw his hand raised briefly in farewell through the back window.

She took the bus home to Mount Victoria where she owned her own small executive flat looking out over the harbour. She ran a bath and yearned for Allen. Your fingers searching, searching, cold yet hot and wanting me, my body. Our mouths joined, tongues molten, saliva dripping, hair and ears and skin, magic in the moment. Bet dried herself thoroughly and took the baby powder canister into the bedroom. She turned back the coverlet and lay down. She lifted up the talc dispenser and began to shake it over her belly. Cool dry powder sprinkled down on her. She shook the talc all over her body and then commenced to rub it into her breasts, belly, groin and underarms. As she did so she imagined Allen doing this with her, her submission to him as he did just exactly what he wanted with her body. Surrendering to him as he aroused her to heights that she had never reached since that year they were lovers, ten years before.

Bet lifted up her hips and tried to imagine his big hard penis thrusting into her aching, lonely cunt. She strained and strained but the vision wouldn't come to her body. She remained miserably alone, physically and mentally, and longed for that tight cosy little single bed she had slept in when she was a child. For her mother to come in and tuck her into bed and kiss her goodnight.

Instead there was a lonely mosquito hum in the cold air, her hottie warm at her side and Allen, you are not here. Not beside me, being secret and hot. I can see you alone under the shower in your flat. Late tonight after sessions are over. How hard your lovely cock is, how sweet, smooth, strong and clean. How you grip it with your big hands and pump it as you think of me, my breasts, my cunt. How I will powder you and wrap you up tight before I love you. Then your sudden spurt, you pant with the release and stand long under the hot water, easing your aches away. We've both had the need. Need for each other unfulfilled and now, we've thrown the dice together, cast our lines in the ocean. What will we catch, what will we score together?

Before she went to work the next day Bet went to Deka and bought two canisters of baby powder, Vaseline, a single flannelette sheet, and a couple of big fluffy cosmetic brushes. She browsed around some more and found some ribbons and bows in pale blue and pink and bought those. Then she suddenly remembered, and went to the baby section and bought two cards of napkin pins, baby soap and muslin washcloths.

At home after work she washed the sheet and arranged the other things in a big basket with fluffy towels and condoms. When the sheet was dry and soft she folded it carefully in a certain way and settled it into the basket. She admired her handiwork and began to wait for Wednesday.

*B*et tried not to be early. She was so excited that she could barely breathe. She was hyped to the max and wondered how she could relax so she and Allen could make love and enjoy exploring all the little treasures she had in her big basket on the back seat of her car. She ran up the path and knocked on the door. Footsteps sounded in the hall and the door was opened by a tall and beautiful blonde woman. 'Hello,' she said in a smooth voice. 'You must be Bet. Mr McDonald is expecting you. Come in.' Bet thanked her lucky stars she had left the basket in the car, covered. Allen appeared down the hall and came to meet her. He held out his hand, smiling.

'Lovely to see you,' he said. 'Jane is making me rehearse my big speech for tomorrow. I've got to be word perfect or she will be cross with me for mangling her lines.' Bet smiled at him. Initially her heart had fallen at the sight of Jane. Perhaps all *will* be well after all she said to herself. Allen showed her into a beautifully decorated lounge. 'Please wait for me here. Have a glass of wine? I won't be long,' he smiled and winked at her as he disappeared out of the room and after a few moments she could hear his voice in full sonorous flight talking about the fiscal balance and the financial deficit.

Bet nervously drank two glasses of wine before Allen had finished with Jane's services and had ushered her out into the evening. He waited at the door until her car had roared away and then shut it with a click and walked quickly in to Bet.

Bet was pacing impatiently, slightly woozy now. Allen wrapped his big arms around her and hugged her. He buried his nose in her hair and smelled her feminine smell.

'Oh Bet,' he sighed. 'You smell like baby powder!' He slid her hand to the front of his suit trousers. She felt his erection nudging her hand. 'Yes, I am pleased to see you,' he laughed. Bet smiled up at him, ecstatic to be safe in his arms once more.

'Now,' Allen said, businesslike, 'I'm going to call a taxi.' Bet went to protest. 'No — don't argue, I know what I'm doing.' He pulled out his cellphone and quickly dialled a number and gave his address. The phone beeped as he hung up. 'Did you bring some things for us?' he asked impishly.

'Yes I did,' admitted Bet. Things were moving too fast for her and her fantasies of making love to Allen in his own bed were evaporating. 'I have a basket out in my car.'

'Good. We'll take it with us when the taxi arrives.' He wrapped his arms around Bet once more and began slowly to kiss her mouth. As he kissed her, Bet unwound to the extent that she began crying, helplessly sobbing into his mouth and Allen held her tighter, sensing she needed closeness. Needed holding until all the tears were gone. Outside a horn tooted and Bet mopped her face and blew her nose on the large tissue Allen offered her. He stepped out and returned with a small case. 'Come on!' he said, 'Taxi's waiting!'

Bet fumbled in her handbag for her keys and got the basket out of her car. Allen gave the taxi an address and they sat quietly side by side, Bet trying not to sniff, as the car sped through the busy, brightly lit city night. It stopped outside a modern apartment complex.

Allen paid the driver and led her to a lift at the back of the building. Native trees hid the entrance from the road. He swiped a plastic card through the lock and the doors swished open. He took out a slip of paper and typed a code into the lift, the doors closed and the lift rose up into the night building.

'This is an empty flat that belongs to a friend of mine. He only uses it for six months of the year and I can use it if I want to when he is away. I can't have you at my flat. For one thing my wife might phone and any one of the other backbenchers might turn up for a nightcap. They do that sometimes. Also, it could be bugged by the SIS. You never know.'

Bet brightened and leaned against him. The lift swished open onto a softly lit corridor with three doors opening off it. Allen led the way to the door at the end, swiped the lock and opened the door. Bet gasped. The room was full of a soft radiance partly from the city lights and the moon outside and partly from the lights glowing from the skirtings of the room. She placed the basket on the floor and gazed for a long time at the beauty of the harbour. Then she turned and hugged Allen.

'Is there a bath here?' she asked.

'I dunno. Let's look,' suggested Allen. The penthouse apartment was luxurious. It had a kitchen-dining room, two bedrooms, a study and a huge living room. There was a large spa bath in the bathroom, a bidet and hair dryer – everything and more than a hotel would have. The kitchen was full of equipment for complex cooking and elegant eating.

The master bedroom had a vast bed already made up with fresh sheets. Velvet curtains framed the windows, swagged aside with huge baroque bows.

'Coffee?' suggested Bet, looking busily through the kitchen cupboards.

'Yes.' Allen's deep voice came from right behind her and startled her. She squealed and kissed him. He had found a drinks cabinet set into the fridge and made himself a whisky and soda. 'Let's relax,' he said. 'Do you want something stronger than coffee?'

'Yes please.' Bet was feeling more secure now, making herself at home. She realised that by meeting at such a neutral place they could be totally free and easy with each other, more so than at her tiny flat or his public one.

They sat looking out at the city and chatting, catching up on old times. Bet alternately sipped her coffee and her wine, relaxing still further until Allen stood up and went into the bathroom. She heard the sounds of running water and smiled, then stretched. I open the doors of our penthouse banqueting hall, she thought. You're here, king of this castle, host of this roast and I tremble with hunger, seeing my long-lust meal standing, bounding, fit and firm before my eyes. I want you so much. With an orca hunger. Bloodied mouthfuls of lust flaming in the pan on our glad fire.

Our hearts, minds, bodies run together. Talking, bargaining. Bargaining this love into lust. 'It's only lust that we share.' A litany of lies. Limiting where all would be given if we could. I want to say, divorce your wife. Live with me. You want to say, be my mistress. Be there when I want you and forget me otherwise. We both want the impossible. Ah, Allen.

Allen came back into the room and said, 'Stand up, Bet. I want to undress you.' He slipped her long black skirt down to the floor, slowly unbuttoned her white blouse and it fell away from her shoulders. He gently lifted her breasts out of her under-wire bra. They still filled his hands and he began to suck on them. It sent shooting ecstasy through Bet's body and down into the innermost recesses of her vagina.

She gasped and sighed. Sighed again. Her heart beat so loudly she felt it would have to be taken out and put under the pillows to quiet it. Allen slipped her pantihose down and kissed her scarcely furred mons. He swung his arms under her shoulders and thighs and lifted her into his arms. She placed her arms around his shoulders and smelled the scent of him as he carried her into the bathroom.

Allen put her down softly beside the bath and tested the

temperature of the water. 'Try it?' he suggested softly. She did and smiled.

'Perfect. May I get in, Daddy?' He was slowly stripping off his suit jacket.

'Yes, my little darling. Get in. Daddy's going to join you tonight for a long play. Is that OK?'

Bet beamed at him. 'Oooh goody!' she clapped her hands as she sat down in the warm bubbly water. She watched as Allen stripped off his tie, white shirt, singlet and underpants. His body was as beautiful and brown as always. His penis was smooth and hard and so sexual that her throat filled with lust as she looked at him.

He stepped into the bath and began to soap her body down, paying particular attention to her breasts, her bottom and her cunt. Bet tingled and sighed, luxuriating in this personal attention she hadn't had in ten years. After she was soaped all over it was Bet's turn to sponge Allen. She got out of the bath and went to her basket where she took out the blue ribbons and the soft washcloth and the baby soap and laid the carefully folded sheet out on the bed with the loose pins beside it.

Allen lay back in the bath, a beatific smile on his face. Bet combed his damp hair and tied the blue ribbons in a sweet bow in the centre. 'That's my darling,' she cooed. Then she washed him all over with the soft cloth, concentrating on his ears and nose, mouth and underarms. 'Now kneel and let mother clean your baby pee-pee,' Bet requested and Allen dutifully knelt in the bath, his erection emerging from the water like a torpedo. Bet slid his foreskin back and licked all around the warm soft head, sucking the loose foreskin into her mouth she explored it with her tongue. Allen moaned softly. Bet stroked the washcloth all over Allen's penis and testicles and bottom.

'Time to get out now darling,' Bet said brightly. 'You dry Mummy and Mummy will dry you.' They towelled each other off, laughing and giggling at themselves.

'Powder time!' crowed Bet, pulling on a towelling robe. She led the way to the bed. 'Now lie down there.' She pointed at the centre of the sheet arrangement spread out on the bed. Baby Allen lay down dutifully with his knees spread wide apart. Bet began to sprinkle baby powder all over his genitals and chest. Then she brushed the powder into his skin crevices with the soft brush.

'Good baby,' she cooed as she stroked and stroked around Allen's testicles and penis. His penis wept clear drops of pre-come onto the powder. Bet leaned down and tasted him. 'Ahhhh!' she shuddered, remembering his taste, the odour of his body. Love flooded through her. She picked up the sides of the nappy and a pin and pulled them tight around his stomach. Allen moaned and began to press his penis up against the soft fabric. 'Lie still for Mummy now,' Bet chided him, his thrusts making it difficult for her to fasten the pin into the fabric.

'Oooh I love my nappy, Mummy,' breathed Allen, his face flushed, his hands clutching the bedspread as his hips moved out of control.

When she had finally fastened four pins into the nappy and it was held tight against Allen's bum Bet sat at the head of the bed and said, 'Now come here darling, it's time for your feed.' Allen crawled up the bed and snuggled into her, almost crushing her beneath him. She moved so his head was supported by her thighs and opened up the robe, exposing her left breast. 'Naaurgh, urgh!' panted Allen. He was impatient. Bet lifted up his head and he began to suckle on her nipple. Immediately Bet's cunt began to flood with desire. Allen sucked for a few minutes and then Bet slid her hand under the nappy and stroked his penis. He stiffened and then cried out around her nipple. Her hand filled with a warm fluid and Bet pulled it out from Allen's nappy. 'You naughty boy! You came on Mummy's hand!'

'Yes Mummy. I couldn't help it,' said Allen in a childish voice. 'You be baby now and I'll be Daddy. OK?' They collapsed in giggles and snuggled down on the bed. Allen wrestled the nappy off and began to brush Bet all over. He brushed her nipples, her buttocks, the backs of her knees and under her arms, he brushed her thighs and her neck. She squirmed and wriggled, moaning softly.

Allen parted her legs and looked closely at her cunt. 'Ahhhh. A wet wee girl we have here,' he said. He rummaged through Bet's basket and found the pink ribbons and the condoms. He tied a ribbon in Bet's pubic hair and another in the curly bangs hanging over her forehead. He stripped open the condom and rolled it expertly down over his penis. Bet watched him, panting, trembling with desire.

Allen sat on the sofa and said, 'Come over here little girl. Daddy's got something for you. Come and sit on Daddy's knee.' Bet sat astride Allen and he opened up her labia, stroking her inner wetness. She gasped as he touched her clitoris over and over again. She desperately wanted to lower herself onto his rigid penis but until he was really ready for her she dared not. Allen sucked her nipples and continued stroking her. Bet moaned and sighed, her labia puffed out and dripping with lust. Finally Allen guided his penis inside her.

They gasped in unison. Bet hyperventilated at the exquisite feelings that Allen's penis gave her as he entered and opened her body right up. Allen picked her up and carried her to the bed where, still inside her, he set her down on the edge of the mattress. Bet lay back, watching his face as he deliberately thrust into her. Slowly the energy between them built until Bet was crying out with each thrust.

'Yess!' she screamed. You thrust into my cunt, transforming my long lonely ache into kinetic energy. 'Thrust, thrust, deeper, deeper, harder, harder . . . oh! God!'

Allen withdrew and turned her over onto her hands and knees on the bed. He grunted as he entered Bet's eager, hungry body once more. He gripped her buttocks and the change of position drove her crazier with the flood of sparkling sensations that filled her body over and over as he withdrew and thrust again and again.

'Oh!' With each thrust you spank my buttocks hard with your big hand and as you spank the cheap glass that is me is thrown against the concrete block wall of my universe and shatters . . . thrust!

Uh! Uh! Uh! Scream hitting a peak as my crystal shatters and shatters and slap aaaaahhhhhh . . . thrust, thrust . . . slap, slap . . . ahhhhhhhh!

More, more, my Oliver Twist body wants you more and more. Oranges squeezed juicy over my forest, grapes in your hair. Oysters unshelled fragrant in your mouth, the salad jungle of sex rustles around us. Your voice and resonant familiarity drown me. You are an immensely strong Oregon timber panel arched taut over me gazing, gazing. Your dark eyes drinking me. Gazing down into my eyes and I am gone again, your bow swooping down through my body, making moan on my strings.

You are hard, masculine. My father and my mother. The power of your will, your lust, your desire for me thrills through me. You are an electric fence, a dentist's drill. A bumblebee in a flower. I am your thing, quivering, longing only to be taken, used, destroyed, made over. My deepest desire, our most absolute hope is that in your taking, my giving, your giving and my taking, from this night on all will be well. Our desperate desire for each other will quit tormenting us.

As you thrust and I shatter over and over again, we are drawn into each other, crying and calling. Primitive birds of prey, animals locked in a death clasp. A clasp which gives life. Ecstasy crescendos upon glory within me and my body tightens around you. Thrusting even deeper you swell and lengthen and with a single triumphant cry loose your sperm into me.

Our bodies taut, gripped like death, I feel in that single moment of stillness your come spurting against my cervix and the enzymes in it flowing in blessed sweet relief throughout my body.

'Damn. Your condom broke,' Bet giggled. 'Just as well I'm on the pill.'

Allen eased his prick out of her and inspected it. The condom was in tatters.

'Shit,' he laughed, embarrassed. 'Sorry darling. Damn

things would break all the time if everyone fucked like we do.' He stripped the rubber off and rubbed his penis over her lips, her face still flushed and lustful. In the delight of aftersex with you I am content to worship you, the essence of you as you rub it over me. The glory of my essence mixed with yours. In this moment I love you more than I have loved you ever before. I collapse on the bed trembling and you lie behind me, whispering words of love in my ear.

'Oh Bet, my sweet motherlover. Oh how I've missed you.'

'Mmmm,' Bet murmured smiling.

'I want all your lust for me,' Allen said, looking deep into Bet's eyes. To make sure of this he pulled a pair of genuine police issue handcuffs from inside his small case which lay beside the bed and locked Bet's hands behind her back. He lay down behind her, covering her, snuggling as close as nature would permit flesh and bone to meld.

'Oh Allen. I love you controlling me like this,' said Bet blissfully. I nestle my handcuffed hands lovingly around your testicles and slowly slackening penis. I close my eyes. With your presence I am in that heaven owned by God and his minions in the churches. I slip silently, quivering, into the dreamless bliss of the saved, the dead, those in heaven, on cloud nine. Only you could do this to me, Allen.

When Bet woke he was gone. So were the handcuffs.

I roll over onto my back and stare at the dark distant

ceiling of this mysterious room. I am alive and so much more alive than before.

You, our heat. Our yeasty smell and the lust of you surround me in the bed. We fill all the room. Just as well no one will be visiting except you much later on tonight. Outside I hear people driving to work. It is time for me to leave.

To go to work and then home. Back to the TV pre-packaged boredom of yesterday. We took a night out of time and my mind is so very clear as I toss my clothes on, pull the bed apart, muss up the room to give the maids a task of interest tomorrow, grab the red carnation you left me, pack up the basket, find my purse and car keys.

Even now, I miss you. Even now, I feel the chill of delight quicken me at the smell of your skin, the murmur of your voice and I shudder as again, as every day for so long, so very very long, I felt you come within me again.

10

$\mathcal{B}$et waited. It was awful. Every time the phone rang at work she thought she would die with anticipation. Allen never called.

Each day a little bit of her died. She cried in the loos, washed her face and imitated cheerfulness to the others. She relied on Louise to help her out, to answer the phone and tell her first who it was. It was always a slow shake of the head, a pursing of her lips as Louise held the phone in her left hand and took notes with the other, her dark hair falling down around her face like curtains of privacy.

It wasn't helped by the fact that everyone seemed edgy, remote, tense, almost snappy. This had never happened before at Tiffany's. Sam seemed cheerful but moody and once Bet found her in the loos crying into the rollertowel. Sam was very close about it all; she said she was living with a woman called Daniella. She wouldn't bring her in to meet them no matter how keenly they urged her to.

Tiffany was pleased about that. Tiffany was jealous of Sam. Sam had been Tiffany's first woman lover and they had shared life and work for almost four years. That made it hard to keep on working together, now they had split. It made it hard for everyone.

On the other hand Tiffany and Louise seemed to have begun a closer relationship but they wouldn't talk about that either. They would laugh together over little secrets; they hugged each other a lot but they weren't really relaxed about it.

Fiona, once Bet's closest friend, was deeply involved with a guy who looked like a long-haired hippie but who was in fact an educated man with a degree and a professional life. Jim had taken Fiona away from Bet and now there was only Louise to confide in.

Once everyone had been open and friendly and supportive at Tiffany's, but now no one was there for you when you crashed because they were all involved in some kind of hurl towards oblivion themselves.

She e-mailed Allen but no answer came. She felt ashamed because his secretary would be reading her begging letters to him and there was nothing she could do about it. She could imagine the secretary getting sick of 'Aunty Glad' e-mailing all the time and putting all her e-mails in the trash can on the desktop or the one more literally beside the desk. Tears sprouted in her eyes again. She rehearsed phoning him in her mind but knew she would have to go through an endless chain of secretaries only to be turned down at the last minute by someone saying coldly, 'I'm sorry, Mr McDonald is in a meeting,' or 'in the House'.

She paged him her new cellphone number. She had bought it especially so Allen could phone her, anytime, any place. It had become her closest friend. It was silent; its beautiful green and red lights flickered regularly but that was all. She gazed into the cellphone's inscrutable virtual face and willed Allen to phone her.

Bet wondered if his wife had to put up with this sort of loneliness too. Allen had his cellphone with him all the time. Bet guessed that only a few people had the number for that. He hadn't given it to her. Maybe his wife used his cellphone to call him?

She rested her hot eyes on her forearm for a while before pulling herself together and looking at the backlog of work which was building up before Christmas. She choked, thinking of another Christmas alone. Allen couldn't help her with that. At parliament the House was under urgency until Christmas Eve and that day he would be flying home to Invercargill to spend eight weeks with wifey and the kids in his electorate. She sighed and the paper in front of her swam. Suddenly she felt very small, alone and neglected.

Being mistress to a politician surely wasn't what she had imagined at all. She had initially seen herself as being taken out to dinner at least once a week. Trysts at expensive hotels, lunch at cafés and long night-time drives. In the last couple of weeks Allen had only managed to get away once in the evening to take her to the ballet. She had loved everything about the performance but he had been too tired to make love with her at their secret penthouse suite.

When we said goodbye I turned to go and suddenly you hugged my coat-clad body from behind. I stood still, midway into departure and all I wanted to do was to turn around, walk back into your life and never leave you for a moment. Why did I leave? Why?

I live and die again in the blissful knowledge that you want me, Allen. I ache deep again knowing another reunion will be followed by another wrench like this one. Each time wrenching deeper into the emotions surrounding us and I cannot outlive this pain, or overbear this longing I have for you. The most sensible path is to turn away, shut the door on you and your glorious sexual athleticism. Block out the deep wet warm of you I love so well overlaid with the swift crust of reason and the rubbery insanity of politics.

But, idiot that I am — I don't block you out. I love you helplessly. When you call I will go to you, driving in joy to our sacred haven of central heating and canned penthouse luxury. To take joy in each other again.

The mouth of one dipping into the wellspring of the other. Coming up full and happy, dripping honey and pavlova. Dropping chippies and apple on the carpet beside the bed. Ordering takeaway scallops juicy and divine in the mouth. Or deep-fried banana melting under the grill and bitten through with intent to do bodily harm. My tongue licking and sucking the banana as it loves to lick and suck your cock.

Fresh from the Palmolive shower you glow wet and dip your fingers into me, tasting my daylong taste and glorying in me, my womanhood. I love you for this. For the true love for women you have. Tenderness, love, genuine honest lust. Truth on the springboard and I jump off. The splash may wet all my life, my love. I cannot forget you and I care so deeply. I've bitten the baited sharp hook of love and now I can't get off. I will never swim free.

Ah. Care, caution, concern, carefulness. The conceit of

love, that we can hide it from our dear ones. Our warmth from those near. How will your wife not know? How will I endure another lonely Christmas without you?

Bet sobbed as she laid her head in her arms on her desk. Louise and Tiffany glanced at each other, concerned. 'It's not looking good — this thing with Allen McDonald,' Tiffany e-mailed Louise. 'I agree,' replied Louise. 'I only hope she doesn't go off the deep end and do something stupid.' Then, hesitating but dying to know, needing to know, Louise asked, 'When can we go to a dungeon?'

Tiffany thought of her daily anguish missing Sam and the open invitation she held in her handbag from Mistress Madeleine. She felt torn apart by the forces of love and grief and work. Perfidy flooded her as she wrote in reply, 'Soon darling, soon'.

♋

Bet drove into her garage and sat silently despairing. She looked at her lovely new car. It would be a good way to go. Easy. Just sitting there. Close the garage door. Tears ran down her face. It seems so long ago that Allen asked me if I could handle it. I said yes, of course I said yes. But I didn't really know what I was saying yes to.

Would I have done it, knowing the agony I'm in now? Yes

— I would. I love him. I've always loved him. Now he's taken away from me by that bloody parliament, by his wife, his family, by Christmas. I've got no one to spend Christmas with. Self-pity filled her to overflowing. The cellphone sitting on the seat beside her blinked and then rang loudly.

Bet jumped and fumbled to open it.

'Hello?' she said desperately.

II

$\mathcal{S}$he was the calm centre of attention in the huge wild snake of the gay Devotion parade as it wound and swam down the crowded streets of Wellington. Perhaps it was because of the four huge, muscular, almost nude hooded male slaves who carried her on her throne. Perhaps it was her flowing priestess robes of jet black velvet with holographic sparkles spangling the darkness. Or maybe the military boots buckled to her small strong feet, thrusting out under her robes.

When anyone looked closer they could see she held in

her hands a long thick leather strop crossed with an open silver and ivory cut-throat razor. At her throat lay a curious piece of gold jewellery she had designed herself . . . 'Labia Possessed', she liked to call it. And if anyone had dared to get closer still they would have seen this jewel mirrored before Madeleine because upon the platform in front of her throne lay the perfect living jewel herself.

Sylvia lay back upon her haunches in an attitude of utmost display and humiliation to which Madeleine had trained her over many loving years. Her long curly blonde hair cascaded around her body, her arms supported her back and a pillow was under her head. Her breasts were covered by a fine silken tissue which did not hide the fact that her nipples were distorted by large metallic silver clips. Her body tingled as thousands of eyes passed over her skin, her lovely hair, her Parisian red-painted lips. It was a punishment Madeleine had made her submit to because she had, she admitted, been a brat that afternoon as they prepared for the parade.

A slick gold mini skirt gripped Sylvia's buttocks and waist, held skintight because her thighs were wide apart, trembling with the fatigue of exposing her jewel to Madeleine constantly over the two-hour parade as she was commanded to do.

Mistress Madeleine had said, 'Feel all those hungry

envious eyes looking at you! They will all want to be where you are. Most of them would do almost anything to be in your position. You are a very, very fortunate slave girl to have my loving correction and care and so, in recognition of this, I am going to insert all your jewels and you will expose them to me and anyone else who gets a glimpse. In addition I want you wet for the whole parade.'

Sylvia was wet indeed. She could feel the slick from her cunt slowly oozing down and soaking into the leather skirt. Was it the tingle of those fat gold labia rings, four on each side, which Madeleine had inserted anew today after a ring-free holiday of four whole weeks? Was it the four tiny but heavy padlocks which fastened those opposing pairs together, thus shutting her vagina against any penetration except from the beloved woman who held the keys? She looked up, thinking of how her cunt in its golden bondage mimicked that lovely ornament Madeleine wore around her neck tonight.

Anyone can see my deepest secret, she thought, shivering in delight. My locked cunt is on display to my mistress and the world! As the slaves walked slowly swaying the litter while the throbbing hypnotic music of the parade vibrated around her she almost came but remembered in time that Madeleine always knew when she had allowed herself to come without permission and that the punishment would be frustrating, traumatic and tiring. With a few deep breaths she fended off the orgasm. She relaxed her muscles as she had been taught and was proud of herself.

Madeleine gazed serenely at the procession in all its wildness pouring past thousands of spectators. She felt immensely proud of her four slaves who were demonstrating their enormous strength by physically carrying her and Sylvia the length of the parade. No other mistress in the city had five such exquisitely well trained and obedient slaves! She was looking forward to the end of the parade because the appreciation of the crowds for her and her little ménage was deeply arousing.

Supplicants and potential slaves ran from the crowd to kneel in front of her and beg her to consider them. Her razored, sparkling eye would strip them naked and she could see in a glance their sincerity or lack of it. If they appeared sincere she would nod and one of the leading slaves would give the prodigal a small black and red printed card which he extracted from his leather codpiece.

She would have a busy week next week. She could feel it in the avid sexual air of the parade. People who never realised they wanted to be submissive would suddenly feel the arousal Sylvia felt as she lay there, open to the world at the command of her mistress, and want it for themselves.

Silently Madeleine thanked those religions which

suppressed and repressed their worshippers. Each group guaranteed her a steady flow of slaves willing to pay dearly and by the hour for her special brand of sexual dominance. She sighed contentedly. It was such a wonderful feeling to find and recognise soulmates in the crowded city streets — people who wanted to dominate or submit and often both. Those delightful switchers! She smiled and twitched her razor and strop.

As the parade dissolved into chaos they found their car waiting. The slaves set down the litter. Madeleine gave Sylvia the command to rise and then, when her trembling cramped limbs would not move, lifted Sylvia's stiff diminutive body up off the litter in her own strong arms and placed her tenderly in the limo. Two slaves sat in front and the other two stood on the running boards each side of the old-fashioned vehicle as it purred away into the hill suburbs.

'What is that for?' asked Louise when Tiffany ran back out of the path of the Devotion parade clutching something to her leather jacket like it was a precious treasure. Tiffany cupped it in her hands and held them in front of Louise. It was a deckle-edged red and black business card.

'You have permission to visit Mistress Madeleine in her

First Class Lounge. I will be at home next week. Please make an appointment with my duty slave. My command is your only wish,' read Louise. 'Oooohhh!' she exclaimed. 'This is your friend who has the dungeon! You mean that . . . that was *her*? In the parade just then? Wow!'

Tiffany grinned and hugged Louise. 'Next week I will go and ask – beg the use of one of her lesser dungeon rooms for our little pleasures,' she said. 'It will cost me but you are worth it.' Louise had her arms around Tiffany's shoulders and their lips met soft and sweet as the wild music of the parade swirled around them. Onlookers began to applaud them as their lips remained glued together. Tiffany's heart beat faster in anticipation. It would do them both good to wait a little longer.

Tiffany began to watch the parade again, Louise on her arm for the first time. Suddenly across the street she saw Sam's blonde spikes unmistakable in the crowd of revellers. She lifted her arms to wave, to try to catch her attention and then her arms fell to her side, numbly.

Unbelieving she stared across the street at the petite bimbo Sam was escorting solicitously through the crowd. A whirl of blonde curls, tiny tight bum, slick gold mini dress, red lipstick, gold eyeshadow over black eyeliner. Naked . . . naked lust in every aspect of Sam's body. Tiffany used to love that, how strong and protective Sam was when she was out with her. So that is what has my Sam, she thought, dazed . . . no wonder she hasn't been home! Not even to get her knickers! Jealousy flamed and froze her inside and out for twenty seconds then vanished, leaving Tiffany limp and feeling terribly alone.

'Did you see that!' exclaimed Louise. 'I thought I saw Sam with another woman. A real femme in a gold mini dress with blonde curls, lipstick, everything!' She looked at Tiffany and saw by her dismayed face that she had in fact seen Sam. 'Oh — I'm sorry. Come on, let's go and get a drink,' suggested Lou and tugged Tiffany away from the rest of the parade as the party people continued to celebrate into the long, hot, moist night.

Tiffany sat blankly and then gulped her wine angrily. Tears began spilling down her face. 'I know why she hasn't brought Daniella to meet us now. Sam still feels ridiculous. Of course it is ridiculous! Being seen with a woman who looks like that. Fancy being taken away from me by a thing like that!' Tiffany laughed bitterly and wiped up her tears with a serviette.

'How could she, of all women, let it happen? Well it couldn't have been rape. I'm sure of that. That bimbo couldn't rape anyone, probably can't even tie up her own shoelaces! I bet she has the biggest wardrobe of trashy clothes anyone has ever seen.'

Louise listened in silence. In the weeks since Sam had left, Tiffany had been anguished but reserved about Sam's defection.

'Why? Why a woman like that instead of me? Why hasn't she phoned me? I have been so worried and we have needed her at work too. Damn it! I have never seen her so unreliable, so out of character. Damn! I miss her.' Sobs caught at her throat and her shoulders shuddered under Louise's arm vainly trying to comfort her.

Oh hell, thought Louise. What will come of Tiffany's now? Will we all be able to stick together after this mess has settled down? Who is that girl Sam was with? At least it doesn't look suspicious Tiff being with me. We have been to Devotion parades before but never without Sam.

Sam felt guilty. She had been standing there pretending to watch the parade but she was really watching Daniella's excitement and the way other people of both sexes looked hungrily at Daniella's delicious body so lightly covered with her mini dress. Sam had seen Tiffany run out in front of Mistress Madeleine and kneel as a supplicant to receive a calling card and run back into the crowd. She knew Tiffany was into the odd bit of bondage and discipline but had never been interested herself. Never followed it up. Not until Daniella had given her a good reason to spank her. Sam smiled at the memory.

Now Tiffany was showing it to . . . who? She peered into the darkness. Daniella's arm tightened about hers as a lewd clown wearing enormous breasts and male genitals flounced in front of them offering free condoms and shaking a coin collection box. Daniella stepped forward delicately in her high heels and dropped two dollars in the box. The clown blew her a kiss and moved down the street.

Yes – it *was* Louise with Tiffany. Louise looked so sweet, so vulnerable and so wildly excited standing there close to Tiffany and reading Mistress Madeleine's card that all of a sudden it came to Sam that Tiffany hadn't really been *in* their relationship for some time. Sam had never guessed. Perhaps it was months or even a year they had kept on living together out of habit. Perhaps it was Louise Tiffany was dreaming about at the disco the night I met Daniella? Hmmm! I bet *that* is why she wouldn't have anything to do with me!

Her guilt evaporating with the help of this illuminating thought Sam turned and smiled down at Daniella.

Something shattered between Tiffany and Sam then, like a crystal loving cup, high in the Himalayan air above the revels of the city. It shattered, bell-like, and left Sam free, utterly free. In that moment Sam realised instinctively that all the ties were broken between herself and Tiffany. Now she could give her energy to her new mistress.

Sam leaned down and kissed Daniella's golden curls. 'The

first time ever I saw your face . . .' she hummed. The shit can hit the fan later, Sam thought as they drifted to the back of the crowd and walked to Constantine's for dinner, I'm not hiding *us* any longer.

12

Once at home Sylvia stiffly got out of the car, helped by Madeleine and they walked slowly to the workout room or her First Class Lounge as Madeleine liked to call it. Once there Madeleine slipped off her velvet robes revealing a leather tunic and full leather pants under the high laced black army boots. The pants were decorated with many zipped pockets as was the tunic which had no sleeves, showing off Madeleine's well developed muscles and allowing for plenty of free arm movement.

The male slaves followed them in and Madeleine

gestured to them. They immediately began massaging Sylvia until she was warm and flexible once more. Madeleine paced up and down the room, ruffling her spiked dark red hair. She had a bunch of tiny golden keys in her hand. When she was ready Sylvia knelt where she was and looked at the floor.

'What do you have to report?' demanded Madeleine sternly, walking across the floor to stand in front of Sylvia.

'Mistress I am wet. Mistress I almost came during the Devotion parade but I did not,' said Sylvia humbly.

'Do you deserve your reward tonight?' demanded Madeleine.

'Yes, sweet mistress, I do,' confirmed Sylvia.

'Beg for it!' Madeleine was merciless.

'Please beloved kind mistress allow me the sweet satisfaction which only your attention can afford me.' Sylvia leaned forward and salaamed at Madeleine's boots nestling in the thick carpet.

'Inspection!' Madeleine took a remote control from one of her pockets and pressed a button. Bright spotlights immediately lit a high table set about with a complex of stands and metallic equipment.

'Permission to stand and move please,' asked Sylvia.

'Permission granted,' said Madeleine softly, walking like a panther to the table. Sylvia moved slowly in her high hobble shoes to the table where she levered herself up onto the chill leather and lay back.

Madeleine lifted Sylvia's legs up into lithotomy clamps which laid her naked pudenda wide open to the bright spotlights. She looked closely at the slick moisture beading the golden locks and rings. She ran her long fingers up under the locks and inspected the fastening of Sylvia's labia. Each piercing she had made herself as a reward to Sylvia for complete obedience. Each piercing had been gained after six months of acceptable behaviour and the complete set represented over four years of fealty with the locks also having to be earned. Madeleine leaned down and ran her tongue over the sweet salty slick metal warmed by Sylvia's body. She smelled so incredibly sweet and sexy.

Madeleine reached out and gestured to the slaves. They melted into the darkness of the four corners of the room where they awaited their own individual rewards. Serving her was reward enough to them all, she knew, but she made sure they also got their pleasures.

Her hand returned holding a feather which she used to stroke Sylvia's inner thighs and labia. Sylvia shuddered and moaned. Madeleine intensified the stroking using her long nails to stripe that tender skin. Sylvia began breathing fast and Madeleine suddenly slapped her on the golden locked pussy. Sylvia cried out and came, shuddering and moaning.

Madeleine moved up the table to speak to Sylvia. 'You came without permission my darling,' she said softly stroking Sylvia's hair. 'You know what that means, don't you?'

'Yes mistress,' said Sylvia faintly.

'What is it to be tonight?'

'We agreed on the water and wax,' said Sylvia trembling. This combination always released more tension and orgasms than any other for her and she suddenly found that the orgasm she had just enjoyed faded into insignificance when compared to what she knew was ahead.

Madeleine took the cut-throat razor and strop from a thigh pocket. She stood beside Sylvia's head, stropping the razor on the fine leather. 'You are a very, very disobedient slave to come without permission and without asking for permission,' she stated loudly. 'As a conscientious mistress I must punish you as you deserve.' She ran the razor up her arm. A fine rain of hair flew out and rained down like dust in the bright spotlights. She leaned in and slid the razor under the fine tissue of the shirt covering Sylvia's breasts and slit it from top to bottom. It fell away from her perfect teacup breasts. The silver nipple clips stood out obscenely; silver teeth crushing Sylvia's tender pink nipples.

The leather skirt followed the shirt and Madeleine beckoned the slaves. They lifted Sylvia off the table and bent her over a high leather-covered bench. Madeleine then fastened Sylvia's wrists and ankles into restraints built into each side of the bench.

The razor was closed and slid away into Madeleine's pocket; the strop folded up and stroked. Sylvia's naked bottom glowed like a perfect peach, its surface interrupted only by a tiny tattoo of a circlet on her left buttock. Suddenly Madeleine moved in and grabbed Sylvia's firm soft skin with her hands. She stroked and massaged and then began to spank her with alternate hands. She spanked until Sylvia's bottom was pink all over and Sylvia was squealing. Then she drew out the strop and began to whip Sylvia with it. Each impact was very loud and Sylvia cried out with every stroke.

After six strokes of the strop on each buttock Madeleine stopped, stretched her shoulders and asked, 'Don't you have something to say?'

'Oh thank you mistress! Thank you for spanking me. I am deeply humbly grateful and I deserved every second of my punishment.' Sylvia was breathless and her pussy was dripping from the locks once more.

The slaves loosed Sylvia from the bench and she was lifted up onto the high chill tabletop once again. Madeleine clicked her fingers and one of the slaves brought her a large bag of warm fluid with a tube attached. She hung it from a stand next to the table, took a rope and tied Sylvia's left wrist to the side of the table. She did the same with the right wrist and then lifted Sylvia's legs, straightened them vertically and tied her ankles to soft cotton ropes hanging from the ceiling for that purpose. Sylvia was now tied with her legs spread lewdly wide.

After walking around the table looking carefully at the way Sylvia was lying, making sure she was straight and as comfortable as possible, Madeleine rearranged Sylvia's hair into a halo around her head and adjusted the nipple clips which had been constricting Sylvia's nipples for several hours. Sylvia squealed as the blood began to circulate in her nipples once again and panted in anticipation as Madeleine made her preparations.

Madeleine changed into a short sarong which was just enough to cover her naked hips and left her big breasts swinging free.

She stood back and considered Sylvia. Certainly a wicked slave and in need of some loving reproof but also the most beautiful treasure and satisfying lover Madeleine had ever had. She took the tube that dangled from the bag and lifted and parted Sylvia's buttocks with her other hand. The tube slid in effortlessly. She looked at the beautiful sight of a loved, locked and helplessly dripping pussy with a tube violating Sylvia's other orifice and said, 'Beg!'

'Please, please mistress allow your special fluid to fill me up completely. I am not fit to clean your boots but please be kind to me and permit me this one pleasure!' Sylvia sounded all there and ready for her ordeal. Madeleine took her bunch of keys and slowly unlocked the padlocks, carefully slipping them out of the rings and hanging them one by one on a rack beside the table. Then she gently slid her fingers inside those wet pink lips and spread them wide. Inside, Sylvia's erect clit could be seen unhooded and throbbing.

Madeleine carefully did not touch it, even though she longed to and instead arranged the fat golden rings so they lay aside, their weight holding Sylvia's vulva open like a gorgeous dew-wet flower.

Then she turned the tap on the tube and the warm fluid began to flow into Sylvia's rectum. Madeleine had perfected a formula which combined a little alcohol, muscle relaxants and stimulants which were absorbed almost at once into the body in this way and she knew that within five minutes Sylvia would be out of control and ready for her.

Madeleine turned aside and lit the candles which the male slaves had placed all around the table. She took a small white candle and stood at the foot of the table once more. The fluid had all drained into Sylvia. Her body was convulsed with the effort of absorbing a litre of liquid. She panted softly and a sheen of sweat covered her silky limbs.

Madeleine slid the tube out of Sylvia and let it drop. She climbed up onto the table and knelt astride Sylvia's face. 'Serve me and make sure you do not lose any of that fluid inside your asshole!' she demanded and Sylvia began greedily to eat Madeleine's wet pussy out.

Madeleine slowly took the nipple clips off Sylvia's nipples and gently massaged them to their normal shape. Then she deliberately dripped a large dollop of hot wax onto each nipple. Sylvia screamed with each drip and clamped down on her anus to keep the precious fluid inside. Her pussy bulged outward, obscenely beautiful in its arousal. Her mouth screaming vibrated Madeleine's clit to within moments of orgasm but Madeleine controlled herself with a supreme effort of will.

She worked down Sylvia's taut stomach, dripping wax in a regular pattern until she reached the blonde curls on the mons of Venus where she put the candle aside. Madeleine leaned forward and began to lick Sylvia's sopping silky pussy until she could bear the tension no longer. She slid off the table leaving Sylvia so near an incredible orgasm that she thought she might die any moment and was almost totally out of control. The drugs surging through her bloodstream made the fluid in her rectum feel enormous and her clit felt like a huge erection but she knew she *must* wait for permission to come or her orgasm would not be considered satisfactory and would be demanded over and over again until she had perfected control.

The hot wax drips burned her skin to unbearable

sensitivity. Her nipples ached warm, matching her bottom which glowed intolerably. After what seemed like an aeon Madeleine was between her legs again and she was holding an unusual instrument. It was a sexual gadget she had designed and made for just these occasions: a three-pronged flexible firm rubber dildo.

One fat sausage slid into Sylvia's anus and increased the pressure unbearably. The second of the matching pair slid tightly into Sylvia's aching cunt. Madeleine held the third erect and lowered herself down upon it with a moan of satisfaction.

Her mouth sought Sylvia's and they rode together to an orgasm which stimulated her four slaves to gather around unbidden with their penises to attention. Without touching themselves, as one organism they spurted in unison with their mistress's orgasm and faded back into the darkness of the room again before she recovered her composure.

'Thank you, mistress,' said Sylvia later in bed as she fell asleep in Madeleine's arms. Madeleine lay awake planning the rewards for her new slaves tomorrow and wondering about the new dominatrixes who would come out of the woodwork in the next weeks as a result of the Devotion parade.

I wonder about that Tiffany, she said to herself as she finally slept.

13

'Hello?' said Bet breathlessly, hoping, hoping it would be Allen.

'Hi Bet, it's Louise. Sorry I'm not Allen.' She paused. Bet's heart sank as always when the phone rang. She was devastated that it wasn't Allen. 'I'm calling to ask if you'd like to join Sampson and me for Christmas? We're going to Palmy to my mum and dad's place. They've got a motel there. Would you like to? I don't know what your plans are. Are you going to go to Invercargill to your mum and dad's for Christmas?'

'Uh – no. I don't think so,' said Bet. 'I've been down there the last couple of Christmases and it's bloody boring.' She was thinking that she didn't want to be that close to Allen and his family. It would just drive her crazy. Crazier than she was now.

'Well – please – come with us,' urged Louise. 'Mum and dad are good fun. They aren't boring at all and there's plenty of room for another person.'

'Um, I'll think about it. Thanks for your invite, Lou.' Bet was retreating. Where to, she did not know. Just backing off. Too tender, too hurt, too lonely to just go somewhere, *anywhere* to have a Christmas. As if Christmas were a fun thing. A thing without significance. The significance of this Christmas for Bet was that she was Allen's lover and she could not be with him. It tormented her like a third-degree burn on her palms.

'The door's always open for you, OK?' said Louise, stubbornly holding out her hand.

'Yeah, I know. Thanks Lou. I'll keep it in mind.' Bet hung up when Louise said goodbye and sat for a few moments longer in her car. She tried to visualise having a Christmas with Louise and her family. With little Sampson it could be fun. The clouds almost lifted. She got out of the car and carried her briefcase up the stairs to the flat.

The cellphone rang loudly in her hand again, just as she

was unlocking the door. She grabbed the briefcase and slammed the door behind her. Allen! It *must* be Allen. She moaned softly, longingly. She could smell him already.

14

$\mathcal{T}$iffany walked in the door of the flat she shared with Sam and wearily put down her purse. Dumping her shopping bags in the kitchen she stared around her. Look at all this, she thought. Sam and I have been so happy here. She wandered around the living room taking in their collection of healing crystals arranged in bowls on the windowsill; Sam's old biker leathers hung on the wall, worn through in the ass and the thighs. Opposite them hung Tiffany's grandmother's watercolours of summer flowers. Tiffany turned and looked out onto their tiny flower-filled courtyard and panicked, asking herself, what will become of our little agency now? Sam pulled the biggest contracts and now she's gone, left me for another woman . . . shit! She kicked the sofa and fell onto it, tears stinging and hot in her eyes. All the work of the last four years was dissolving like the wicked witch of the west into a pool of shit and fuck-nothing before her eyes. Angrily she sat up and tugged her long wild curls free of her ponytail.

I should give us credit for coming a long way, she thought as she unlaced her boots and threw them one at a time at the door. They made loud bangs on the woodwork but no one would hear, no one would care. Sam would care if she was here, thought Tiffany sadly. She crawled over to their music cabinet and looked at the CD collection climbing into the air above her in black architectural steel splendour. She chose a CD and put it on.

The first time . . . ever I saw your face . . . Roberta Flack crooned softly.

It had all begun at that Qantas Christmas do they held at the zoo. Tiffany managed to get admitted as a friend-of-a-friend's good-looking girlfriend. Yeah — *not*. The guy was boring but the bash promised to be interesting which was why Tiffany had wanted to get in. It was a million-dollar party hosting a thousand of the loaded and joyful. After wandering around for a while enjoying the scenes going down, the live music and the wild way the animals responded it, Tiffany got hungry and went over to the buffet.

There was a tall woman with cropped blonde hair standing at the buffet eating — eating messily with her fingers, squishing the food together in fistfuls like a year-old child. She was holding the food out away from the black leather waistcoat and biker pants she wore. A pile of food scraps grew in front of her black-booted feet. Staring at Tiffany, she swayed to the slowest beat of the samba and smiled, still eating. Ostentatiously sucking her fingers, she looked Tiffany in the eye then down at the sticky mess of her hands as if she had never seen her fingers this way before. *I thought the sun rose in your eyes . . .*

Suddenly Tiffany found she couldn't breathe. She stared at this blonde, spiky, bejewelled, leathered, almost masculine-seeming woman. What was it about her that was so mesmerising? Something about the way she was eating? Moving her lips and jaws, her wide smile full of perfect teeth? Her deep blue eyes? Those sticky fingers? Tiffany looked down at the food, trembling, overcome with her beauty. Lusting for her.

Shocked, but lusting all the same. The feeling was unmistakable. A strong desire to kiss that lovely white neck. It would be divinely perfumed by her body odour. Suddenly Tiffany had an aching need to discover those breasts that peeked pertly out through the soft leather waistcoat, unhampered by a bra, swelling visibly into a cleavage. To explore those earlobes with all those kinky silver earrings in them . . . feel those long leather-clad thighs against hers . . . *and the moon and stars were the gifts . . . you gave.*

Tiffany decided to fill her plate and drag her eyes away from that compelling woman. There among the pavlova and pastries, olives and guacamole was a big dish of custard squares! Thick golden egg custard sandwiched between crisp pastry, dripping with heavy white frosting. Her favourite! She was about to choose one when a muscular pale arm reached under her palm, brushing her hand with electricity, picked up the custard square Tiffany had selected and sailed it away.

'Excuse me!' Tiffany said, miffed.

'Sorry, did you want that one?' asked the blonde, grinning at Tiffany, looking her right in the eye.

'Yes — I did!' Tiffany was flustered. She reached for another custard square. Bugger the savouries, she thought, diet down the drain for a week, I don't care. You only get to a party like this occasionally.

'I see you like them as much as I do?' The blonde smiled warmly, her long fingers pulling gooey pieces off the custard square and popping them into her mouth.

'Yes, they're my favourite.' Not all custard squares are

equal, Tiffany thought, her hand hovering, trembling, trying to decide. The woman had put her off.

'Try a piece of mine.' The blonde held out two fingers plastered with custard, pastry and icing. Held them in front of Tiffany's mouth. Tiffany's knees became weak, her stomach flip-flopped and she swallowed. Sweat broke out all over her body as she looked at those inviting sexy fingers and longed to have them deep in her mouth. The intense blue eyes behind the fingers looked hotter than any blue should be.

To the dark and the endless skies, my love . . . 'Go on.' The woman's voice was husky and deep now, under the beat of the band. She laid a fingertip on Tiffany's lower lip. Tiffany let her jaw drop and the custard-covered fingers slid in where she could suck them. She did; oh she did! Sucking hungrily, feeling faint with desire, weak, languorous and horny.

Tiffany pulled herself together and took the fingers out of her mouth. They hadn't wanted to leave. 'Uh – thanks. Delicious. What's your name?'

'Sam,' said the woman wiping her hands on a serviette.

'Do you always feed strangers like that, Sam?' asked Tiffany.

'No, usually only myself,' she said calmly. Her eyes were intense and seemed to be telling Tiffany a lot of things her mouth wasn't saying. 'What's your name?'

'Tiffany, I'm a friend of a friend of — it doesn't matter,' she finished weakly, waving her hand vaguely in the direction of the furthest corner of the party. Tiffany reached out again for a custard square. The fingerful she sucked from Sam had whetted her appetite for more. *To the dark and the endless skies, my love.*

'Would you like coffee and somewhere quiet to talk?' asked Sam.

How could she echo Tiffany's thoughts so exactly? 'Yes! that'd be great!' She smiled up at Sam feeling attracted, at ease and fascinated all at the same time.

Sam led the way, instinctively following a high chain fence that led into the warm darkness of the zoo. The party noise faded behind them. They passed couples engaged in intimate talk separated at discreet intervals down the fence. Sam kept walking. Tiffany followed clutching a black coffee and her plate supporting three custard squares.

Then Sam asked, 'Will this do?' indicating an unoccupied seat off the path under some trees. It was almost invisible in the darkness. Immediately Tiffany's heart beat faster at the thought of solitude and Sam.

'Yes, it'll be fine,' she said quietly, jubilant. Sam sat down and patted the wood beside her. She was smiling, breathtakingly beautiful, or was it just the light? Her teeth were a delight and her jawline was strong and wonderful. Her vanilla-bean mouth was iridescent purple in the dimness. As Tiffany sat beside her, Sam asked, 'May I feed you your custard squares? I'd like to, if you'd like me to.'

'I'd love that!' Tiffany astonished herself but it was the truth. She abandoned herself to the exquisite feeling of being fed, tenderly fed sweet crunchy creaminess from those lovely long fingers. Tiffany ran her teeth gently along them, curling her tongue between them, stimulating the sensitive edges of the digits as a repayment for bliss.

Then her eyes closed and she slipped slowly deeper into the savour of Sam as instead of fingers, a soft mouth gently nibbled her lips and a tongue traced the outline of her mouth. *The first time ever I kissed your mouth . . .*

'Mhhhh . . . Oh . . . Sam . . .' Tiffany was gone, into a heaven of sensual pleasure. Her breasts were touched into stunning sensitivity as gold, onyx and blue flashed in front of her eyes. Little moans escaped Tiffany as Sam played her nipples expertly. Sam's mouth engulfed Tiffany's lipstick-clad lips and drank from them. Heat poured through Tiffany's body from Sam. Suddenly she felt the meaning of true passion.

She lifted her hips so Sam could slip off her pants and panties and then, in an instant, Sam was kneeling between Tiffany's thighs.

A part of Tiffany freaked out. Help, help, help! I don't want this! What am I doing with a woman? I should be here with a man!' But the pleasure was so exquisite she realised a man had never given her feelings like this. Never such passion, appreciation, tenderness, sensuality, custard squares. *I felt the earth move in my hands like the trembling heart of a captive bird that was there at my command, my love.*

Sam opened her waistcoat. Tiffany ecstatically stroked and sucked Sam's delicious softly swelling breasts and nipples as Sam lay over her, a satin passionate coverlet gorgeously warm. Tiffany let her hands stray all over Sam's body. Delicious hollow buttocks, long, lithe, strong legs. The zipper on her leather pants ran around to the back of the crotch and Sam had unzipped it. Now her wet cunt was pressed onto Tiffany's thigh and Sam's leather-clad thigh pressed deep and hard between Tiffany's legs.

There at my command, my love . . . Sam made circles of kisses. Nipple, mouth, nipple. Nipple — mouth, around and around. Tiffany came the first time shuddering and sighing, out of control, lost and loving every moment. Then Sam slid her fingers into Tiffany's wet cunt and rubbed her thumb over her clit and soon Tiffany came again, biting her hand blue so as not to scream out in her pleasure. Shuddering, trembling, panting. Fucked, and by a woman.

The first time ever I lay with you, I felt your heart so close to mine . . . Sam held her snug until the waves calmed.

Gently kissing her, stroking her body and hair. Murmuring soft loving things to each other. Tiffany slid between Sam's legs. Lifted and parted them finding that lovely forbidden frilled delicacy. Seafood on the buffet, escargot, avocado. Eagerly burying her face in womanhood as if this were her everyday experience. Sam seemed in heaven as much as Tiffany was and cried out so loud Tiffany was afraid they'd be heard by the couples down the fence towards the party. Never mind, the party was still going; a band was playing Sinead O'Connor, no one would know the difference.

And I knew our joy would fill the earth and last . . . till the end of time, my love. Delicately, tenderly Tiffany stimulated Sam, trying to repay pleasure for pleasure until 'Stop! Stop! . . . ahhh, ahhh, ahhh!' Sam subsided into a panting, shuddering, sweating tangle of limbs. Tiffany sat back on her heels panting, grinning. That was so much more satisfying than helping a man to come.

They smiled, laughed and snuggled up together leaving damp patches on the timber seat. 'I'm so glad I found you!' Tiffany laughed. 'I was sure I'd die of boredom.'

'Me too, honey pie,' Sam chuckled wiping Tiffany's mouth with a serviette. 'Thank you for a lovely party, we must try this again some time.'

'I've never done this before, you know,' Tiffany put on her serious voice.

'Always a first time for everything, but you're pretty damn good for a novice.' Sam raised one eyebrow at her in a way Tiffany came to adore. They dressed again. Tiffany tried vainly to restore some order to her long red ringlets. They ate the rest of the custard squares together, drank the cold coffee and talked and talked until Tiffany looked at her watch and said, 'Oh God – I'd better get back, someone will wonder what has happened to me.'

'Where do you live?' Sam urgently wanted to know. Tiffany gave her a business card made at the five-dollar machine. They arranged to walk together along the waterfront the next day.

Dressed and with her lipstick back on the only difference was inside herself. Tiffany slipped back into the still-raging party. She checked and found she hadn't been missed at all but now, for some reason, she felt like dancing and danced alone in the midst of the crowd until Sam found her and jived slowly, languorously for the rest of the night near her, bumping asses, breasts, arms or thighs whenever they could.

15

$\mathcal{S}$o there it is, Sam. You joined the perfect symmetry of custard squares in my life. I remember I once told you about my lifetime of custard square coincidences. Your hair was golden in the sun. Cut short but not spiked or dyed yet. Your earrings blinded me with their silver sparkle. Your eyes unfathomable behind your black wraparound sunglasses. The Victoria Café make their own delicious custard squares. We bit together into the piquant sweetness of the perfect soft white icing laid palette-knife thick and fluffy over the pastry and down into the firm delicious custard deeply layered underneath. Finally we scrunched into the other half of the flaky pastry which keeps the whole together in the form of a cake. A divine, dangerous, bacteria-filled confection. As always you pulled your custard square apart with your long sexy fingers and my heart flip-flopped.

My mother loved custard squares and made her own version using Sao crackers laid in a grid on the bottom of a sponge roll tin, instead of making pastry. Then she would make the thick custard herself. Pour the viscous hot liquid, steaming vanilla orchid perfume, over the biscuits and place another layer of crackers over the bright yellow egg-shiny surface. Then she would mix a little hot water and butter into the icing sugar and cocoa, making thick chocolate icing which she spread on top of the crackers. My brothers and sisters and I would all clamour to lick the icing and custard bowls and they would have to be fairly shared out or tears would result. Then we'd forget the custard squares until teatime when mum would bring them out to the table and serve us each a generous helping. Mum was never ungenerous with what she liked.

Perhaps that is where the story would end for most people. But my first lover also craved custard squares and we would buy one each of huge size from our favourite shop on the corner. We'd take them on picnics where we would eat them ritually after making love on the deep leaf mould in the bush. He'd smoke and drink beer and watch me bathing in the chill green mountain stream before we returned to the city, mother of our custard squares.

Eventually we parted and now, on the odd occasions when I visit him, I take two custard squares for us to share along with his thermos of tea in the garden. He laughs his mellow laugh and we reminisce about our past custard square romantic adventures. Kawhia hunting for fossils. Coromandel camping under the red rain of pohutukawa flowers, staining the green canvas of the ancient tent red. The icy cold of Invercargill and the superb warm fresh custard squares we once bought there. The white lemon icing just slightly liquid and melting off the top.

I introduced my nephews to custard squares last year. We made them with sheets of pastry bought from the supermarket. We had enormous fun filling a flat dish with the soggy, clammy pastry, rolled out into flattened lumps by two little boys. Baking it flat, crisp and sugary. Heating the milk and watching the magic as the custard powder, egg and sugar mixture thickened under the whisk in the scalding milk. Waiting patiently until the custard was cool enough to pour on top of the waiting pastry. Then measuring out eight tablespoons of icing sugar to make the icing. Adding pure fresh lemon juice. Not as creamy as butter icing but so pure tangy-tasting I can't help making it for everything.

Chasing each other around the kitchen with the whisk and the icing bowl and arguing over who fairly gets which utensil to lick and slobber over until there's no washing up to do.

And now you, Sam. I marvel at us. Such coincidences are too great to be ignored yet what possible meaning do custard squares have in my life except as fattening desserts combined with delicious sexual adventure?

Sam shakes her head in mute answer and eats her custard square with her fingers, messily as usual. Killing me with love and lust she feeds my greedy mouth from her long sexy fingers in full view of the staid and disapproving Wellingtonians quietly sipping their tea and munching foccacia.

> *last till the end of time . . . my love . . .*
> *The first time ever I saw . . .*
> *your face . . .*
> *your face . . .*
> *your face . . .*

Tiffany's face was wet with tears as Roberta Flack's voice faded into the background and she sobbed uncontrollably, wanting and missing Sam. Sweet strong Samantha. Her strength, her support, her loving . . . gone . . . her face, till the end of time . . .

There were heavy footsteps at the door and a knock. Tiffany scrambled to her feet, dashing tears from her eyes. After a few seconds she felt composed enough to answer the door, hoping it wasn't the Blind Foundation wanting a donation. She'd hate them catching her crying, a tear-stained face peering around the door in the middle of the day like an abused housewife.

Sam was standing there, bulky and shy on the doorstep. 'Sam!' cried Tiffany, overjoyed and wondering why, after all this time, Sam would show up now. 'Come in,' Tiffany stood aside from the door and Sam walked over to perch nervously on the edge of the sofa. She held a brown paper bag in her hands. Roberta Flack crooned on in the background with the rest of her album. Sam gestured towards the stereo. 'Playing our music?'

Tears filled Tiffany's eyes again. 'Yeah,' she said softly. 'It looks like you are with that blonde girl now and our relationship's finished. I was just remembering . . . you know . . . custard squares . . . how we met? Sort of trying to let go of you, since you seem to be gone.'

Sam hung her head and when she lifted it again there were tears in her eyes too. 'Tiff . . .?' she said hesitantly. 'I brought you something.' She held out the bag. 'For old times' sake, eh?'

Tiffany took the bag and opened it. Inside were two

custard squares stuck to each other with their icing oozing out. She screamed in delight, then wiped her eyes, giggling and sobbing all at once.

'You silly romantic bitch,' she said fondly to Sam. 'Do you want a coffee with yours?'

As they were eating and drinking Sam said, 'Something weird has happened to me, Tiff. Over the last few weeks. I would never have believed it could happen – except it has.' She chuckled at herself. 'I met Daniella. It started as lust, just frustrated lust. But now I'm in love with him.' Sam glanced at Tiffany.

Tiffany frowned in bewilderment. 'What do you mean . . . ? In love with HIM?' her voice rising in panic. 'Daniella's the most feminine bundle of womanhood I have ever seen!'

'Yeah, she's that all right. But she's also actually a man. With a penis and balls . . . and fertile.'

Tiffany sat opposite Sam, stunned. She looked hard at Sam, wanting her to be lying, wanting this wild turn of events to vanish, disappear. But Sam looked calm, happy even . . . shit!

'My God!' whispered Tiffany. 'That – that little blonde is really a bloke? Well I would never have guessed! Never! How old is he? Or do we call him she?'

'She's twenty years old and she thought I was a man!'

Sam chuckled throatily and Tiffany began to laugh at the irony of it all.

'You mean?' she cackled . . . 'You mean when you met; *you* thought she was a girl and *he* thought you were a man! Jeez!' Tiffany lay back in the armchair and laughed and laughed and laughed. Coughing and catching her breath. Then she ran to the bathroom before she peed her pants. Sam sat there, twiddling with her earrings, occasionally chuckling at the idiocies of life, waiting until Tiffany was worn out.

'Wild but true. And I love her, Tiff, I really do.' Tiffany looked across at Sam. The words still felt like stabs to her heart.

'What are you gonna do? All your friends are women. Hell! They only know you as a butch lesbian?'

Sam grinned, 'Well, they'll just have to get used to me and Daniella because we are going to be an item for quite a while. We have discovered that we can pleasure each other in ways we didn't know the opposite sex could achieve.' She paused. 'Also — I'm pregnant.'

Tiffany slumped in her chair, wide-eyed, horrified.

'How the hell did that happen?' she whispered.

'The usual way,' said Sam softly, grinning. 'No IVF or artificial insemination. The first prick that enters my body, I don't even know it *is* a prick inside me, and it makes me pregnant.' She paused. Tiffany seemed about to speak and Sam continued, 'No, I'm not gonna have an abortion either.'

'Are you going to carry on working at Tiffany's? We need you for the Art Gallery contract if nothing else. *I* need you!' Tiffany was desperate, her hands pulling tissues to threads, the pieces snowing down onto the floor in front of her.

'I do want to stay on with Tiffany's. After all it is *our* business and we have built it up together. It's seriously profitable so why should we abandon it now? Daniella has a good job and will support me while the baby is very small but I will keep on working several days a week and from home and there's always daycare.'

Tiffany looked at Sam, tried to imagine her trim figure bulging with pregnancy and just couldn't. 'Wow,' she whispered, 'this is just so . . . wild, so unexpected.' Sam shook her head ruefully. 'It's going to take me some time to get used to this new image of yours,' said Tiffany. 'And Lou, Bet and Fiona are gonna be blown away.'

'Let me tell them Tiff, I'd rather do it myself. But I thought you should know first.'

'Thanks.' Tiffany looked up at Sam. 'When are you gonna come and get your things? We'd better split our stuff up sometime.'

'I'll come around this weekend, if that's OK with you?'

'Yeah. I'll be here. It won't be easy to do this, Sam.'

Tiffany was hugging herself, sitting on the floor, rocking back and forth.

Sam wiped her eyes and said gruffly, 'It's not easy and I'm not exactly thrilled with the idea of living with a man or having a child myself. I didn't see my life mapped out like this. But – there it is. I refuse to go down the abortion path. This child got itself conceived while it's mother didn't even realise it had a chance to get going. If it's that wily it deserves to live and I'll go through with the whole deal for it to have a life.

'That's really brave of you, Sam,' said Tiffany, getting up and hugging her.

'It doesn't feel brave,' said Sam. 'Just really scary and inevitable. Like death, almost.'

16

'*B*et?' Allen sounded distant, harried and very tired.
'Darling, how are you?'

She laughed happily, transformed in a moment from a
lump of misery into a joyous being. 'I'm — I'm fine, just *fine!*'
she said. 'When can I see you?' Biting your bait. The sweet
taste of your voice. The promise of you soon, sometime soon.

'I am calling to apologise for the last few weeks. I just
haven't had time to phone you. I'm sure you've heard the
news. About the huge piles of legislation we had to pass
in the House before the Christmas break?' His voice was

desperate for understanding. A reluctant fisherman today.

'Yes, I know. I've been listening. Your speech was repeated on the radio,' said Bet proudly. 'It was great!'

'Thanks,' he said. 'Darling, I just haven't got any time to see you before I fly out tomorrow to go home. I'm really sorry. I've been hanging out to see you but I'm wasted by the schedule we've had. I've hardly had any sleep. I've got to go home to the wife and kids and sleep for a week.'

Bet's heart crashed, burning out in the atmosphere. She leaned against the kitchen wall. There were no words, only the anguish of the solid hook lodged deep in her gut, the fishing line of love bloodily ripping up her mouth as she spun, flipping, fluttering, around and around in sickening, dizzying circles. Struggling to get free. Caught.

'Bet?' he asked, anxiously. 'Bet?' She mustered her energy slowly and drew a couple of deep breaths.

'I'm here,' she said. *Allen!* she screamed inside her head. She held on with a huge effort. He must not know. Must never know.

'Please understand, darling,' Allen pleaded.

'I know, I can handle it. I told you I could and I will.' Bet didn't sound convinced, even to herself. 'I'm really disappointed too,' she said, dissolving into tears. 'Oh God! When can I see you again? When?' Desperately she grabbed a paper towel and blew her nose.

'I'm not due back in Wellington until February at the earliest,' he said. Bet had known this, the length of the recess. She knew Allen acutely needed a holiday but the small inner part of herself which needed loving cried out. 'What about me, what about me? Do I get nothing?' and it was like Allen was saying over and over, 'Nothing. I have nothing to give you Bet. Nothing.'

'Well — I — I'll see you then,' Bet imitated a brightness that was as false as her hair colour. 'I miss you Allen. I love you.' Now she was honest and the relief was extreme.

'I love you too, Bet. Darling, I love you.' He paused and there was a loud noise in the background. He covered the mouthpiece of the phone. When he came back on, the noise was of a loud drunken party. 'Look — I've gotta go. I'll call you when I can. OK?'

'OK,' said Bet softly. 'Bye.' The phone hissed and was dead in her hand. She threw it across the room. If she had felt lonely before, she was even more lonely now. She sank to the floor and screamed, and screamed, and screamed.

17

$\mathcal{T}$he conference was at the Aotea Centre. While Jim was ensconced in boring lectures and discussions in the Hauraki Room, Fiona wandered around the conference complex thinking about him, wanting him all the more because he was unobtainable, remembering his hand on her thigh, his soft loving kisses on the flight to Auckland. Her breasts throbbed.

That morning she had stood in the bathroom looking at the result of her pregnancy test and she wasn't surprised it was positive. She felt the presence of her mother in that moment. How delighted mum would be at having a grandchild after ten years without one! All her mum's friends had grandkids and now her mum would have something to skite about too.

I wonder what mum felt when she found she was pregnant with me? She smiled softly. I must ask her.

Her body felt truly alive, growing, changing, evolving with the child. Already her breasts were fuller, darker; her body more sensitive. She found her sex responding more sensitively to Jim's every touch and she discovered he was even more loving and attentive to her now she was pregnant.

Restlessly she ran up and down the stairs between the levels of the conference centre and wandered on the outside balconies. She lay down in the sun and watched Aotea Square. Below her the skateboarders showed off their moves. Fiona grinned and gasped as they flipped their boards, took leaps and bounds into the air over the concrete. Disaster was only inches away. They flew down steps, ricocheted up onto the slopes of the sculpture that erupted from the paving of the plaza and back again. Rocket-propelled by body, gravity, energy. Flight on wheels.

Suddenly cool hands slid up her toasting legs and a body covered her in a press-up. Fiona froze until Jim breathed into her ear, 'Hi beautiful, how's the most gorgeous woman in the world?' His hand found the bottom of her mini skirt and slipped up towards her panties.

'My sexy Fiona, how would you like to have your wicked way with a horny lonely conference member?'

Fiona laughed. 'What? Have sex here? In the Aotea Centre? This is the most un-sexy place in the whole of New Zealand to have a fuck.' She rolled over, slid her hands down the front of Jim's pants and there, sure enough was his hard-on. Lust struck her below the belt. 'OK — yeah, I'm ready if you are,' she giggled. 'Where could we?'

'Come on, let's have a look. We'll find something,' said Jim. Holding hands they walked into the Maunganui Room. The centrepiece was a huge well in the floor. Below them sounded the sonorous tones of the guest speaker at the conference. The room was in darkness save for the light reflecting up from the conference room. Fiona leaned against the railing and looked down at the audience.

You unlucky boring bastards! Jim's hands slid up under her blouse and his deft fingers began stroking her breasts. She sighed and slid against his strong body, his erection pressing firmly into her buttocks. She almost moaned. Her cunt flooded at the thought of what they were doing above the heads of salesmen, reps and professionals gathered together in the name of Insurance.

Fiona idly listened as Jim unzipped his pants and pulled

his penis out. She reached behind her and touched him with the tips of her fingers. She loved how his cock always felt — so very warm. It was hot, really. She melted under Jim's hands and began eagerly sliding his prick inside her panties. He suddenly withdrew and said, 'No. Not now. Lean back against me,' putting his penis away inside his pants again.

She sighed in disappointment. Jim reached once more for her nipples and concentrated on stroking them softly, then firmly, scrubbing them with his fingernails, until she was begging for him to fuck her. 'Please, please darling, please just for a minute, put him inside me. Please,' she whispered.

'No, there's a man watching us over there,' he whispered back, laughing softly. 'You must wait. Come on. Let's find a better spot.' Fiona looked at the shadowy watcher on the other side of the room and frowned. I hope he doesn't follow us, she thought.

They slunk through the Kaikoura Room which was silent and in semi-darkness. The bar was empty, obviously not being used for the conference. Fiona went into the ladies' loos and decided that while they were comfortably carpeted and mirrored that there was no real privacy to be found there. She walked slightly uncomfortably, her labia swollen and wet. She gazed at herself in the mirror, took out her lipstick and slowly re-applied it, imagining running Jim's penis around her lips in just the same way. Licking his pre-come off the tip . . . mmmmmmm. She stuck her tongue out and licked the tip of her lipstick by mistake and coated her tongue with pink. 'Urgh,' she mumbled and spat it out. She wiped her tongue and teeth with a tissue and had to begin again with the lipstick. Swoop, up to the centre of the top lip, swipe, down to the corner and mmmm along the lower lip, trembling in anticipation.

Her cheeks were glowing, eyes sparkling. She realised she was blooming as she had never done before. Fiona stood back and regarded herself, placed her hands over her belly. Then she smiled and walked out to her lover, dancing on the way to the tune of her joy.

'There's a screen over there,' whispered Jim. 'If it was enclosing empty space it would have been ideal but there's a big stack of folding chairs and tables hidden behind it.'

Fiona put her arm around Jim's waist. 'Never mind. Let's go down to the foyer and look at the Christmas trees.' They spent some time walking around admiring the trees. Each tree had the name of a school underneath it. Fluffy cottonwool sheep and painted cottage cheese pottle tops glittered and swung from the trees. It was a nice contrast to the glitzy storefronts in the city.

Fiona sat down on one of the wide leather seats facing the John Dory tapestry. Jim sat opposite her. The fish looked down on them, grinning hungrily. Fiona pulled up her mini skirt and parted her legs. Suddenly Jim realised that she wasn't wearing any panties. He blushed, and looked over her shoulder at the foyer. Some people were wandering by but no one appeared interested in them.

Fiona put her left index finger into her pussy cleft and began to slide it up and down in her slick moisture. She smiled at Jim and saw his erection leap up in his pants again. He crossed his legs in an effort to hide it. Fiona was delighted. She no longer cared if anyone saw her being lewd with Jim. She was revelling in being an exhibitionist and in the Aotea Centre! That great sterile white whale stranded in the centre of Auckland! She giggled with joy and wriggled forward, parting her legs wider so Jim could see her fig split wide open and juicy. Jim stared hungrily, licked his lips and glanced away into the big room. He looked hot underneath his beard. He clasped his hands together and wriggled around on his seat.

'That guy is watching us!' he hissed. 'Fiona!' She giggled and sat up, sliding her skirt down modestly, primly smoothing it across her thighs. She didn't believe him for a minute.

'Come into the Ladies with me,' she said, beckoning. The toilets were divided into luxurious rooms, the largest entirely carpeted and mirrored. A wide bench encircled the room under the mirrors. Impatient to begin Jim lifted her up onto the bench and knelt in front of her, parted her thighs and began licking her clit. Fiona sagged back against the mirror and let the sensations of his tongue send her ever nearer the golden lip of orgasm. She sighed and panted.

The door opened and a woman carrying a bucket and mop entered the room. She stood there, arms akimbo, shocked, and said loudly, 'I suggest you two get out of here fast before I call security.' Jim started and pulled away from Fiona. Fiona blushed and slid down off the bench, pulling her skirt down.

'Sorry,' was all Fiona could think to say and they scuttled out into the foyer. They hurried over to the lifts and collapsed laughing behind two big Christmas trees. Jim was weeping with laughter and hiccuping. Fiona got a fit of the giggles and had to sit down on the floor. People were moving through the corridor and looked at them sternly. 'No silly laughter allowed in the Aotea Centre — puh-lease!' Fiona felt the need to escape. She was hot and trembling and her body ached for the continuation of what they had begun. She studied the diagrams beside the lifts. 'Let's go all the way! Let's go to the fifth floor!' she suggested.

'There's gotta be a private place to have sex somewhere here,' muttered Jim. 'There's just gotta be.' They wandered about, hand in hand, in the silence of the fifth floor. No one seemed to be around. They looked at the photographic exhibition on display. Hidden behind a group of exhibition screens Jim caught Fiona to him and kissed her passionately. She loved the smell of her sex on his lips. He slid her mini skirt up to her hips and she undid his fly and took out his rigid penis. He lifted her up in his arms and she slid onto his penis. Cooing ecstatically, Fiona rode him. Jim thrust into her slowly, holding her up in his strong arms. Suddenly he froze. 'What's wrong?' asked Fiona, clinging to him.

'That bloody man is watching us again!' he whispered.

'What man?' Fiona felt wild with desire and frustration and excitement.

'He's playing with his prick, the dirty bastard.' Jim set Fiona down and she pulled down her skirt. She felt empty without him inside her.

Jim strode out from behind the screens and said loudly, 'Piss off you sneaky bastard!' She heard the sound of running footsteps. 'He's gone,' said Jim, coming back and putting his arms around Fiona. 'This is getting to be a real drag. What are we going to do?'

'Here's a dark nook,' said Fiona. 'It's the loos!' she said after peering around. 'I'm going to go in the disabled loo, I like them.' She walked into the room and locked the door. Ahead of her another door opened into the toilet itself. Wow! Here it was! The best place for a fuck they could ever find in a public building! A large private toilet and small lockable carpeted room next to it, ideal for sex if anyone thought the way they did. Fiona rushed to the door and unlocked it. Jim was leaning against the wall, waiting, his arms folded, brows creased. Even his beard seemed frustrated.

'Come in!' hissed Fiona. 'Come on!' Jim raised his brows. 'Yeah?'

'Yeah,' said Fiona. Jim couldn't believe it either, a luxury fornicatorium with locking door, carpet and toilet. Fiona locked the door behind him and stood there grinning. Slowly she stripped off her blouse, her bra and then her mini skirt. Flames leapt through Jim's body. He pressed Fiona to the wall and engulfed her mouth with his. He gripped her hips to him and humped against her, moaning, grunting like an animal. Fiona exalted in his loss of control. She drank in his masculinity; delighted in his lust. She began stripping him, unzipped his fly, fumbled with the button, thrust his underpants and pants down, down, as far as she could reach. Began unbuttoning his shirt so she could feel his soft warm furry chest against her tender breasts.

'Lie down,' Fiona said, 'Lie down.' Jim lay on the carpeted floor and Fiona knelt astride him. She looked down at him and smiled. He is my universe, she thought, all I could ever need. His hands strayed all over her body, tweaked her nipples, stroked her back; she gripped his penis and rubbed it over and over her wet labia. Finally she allowed him to slide within her then she leaned forward and kissed him deeply as she rode him. In a few moments he came inside her, moaning into her mouth.

'Oh God,' he said. 'Sorry. I just couldn't hold on any longer.'

Fiona smiled.

'I didn't expect you to,' she said.

18

$\mathcal{T}$he phone rang six times and then the answerphone picked it up. 'Tiffany here. I'm not –' Louise hung up, frustrated. 'Damn! Where is she?' She pressed redial and listened impatiently to the rings not being answered. Then she dialled another number which just rang and rang. No answer, no answerphone either.

'Shit! I wanted to ask Bet again if she was going to come up to Palmerston North with me.' She put the phone down and turned away. It rang loudly. Louise jumped in surprise, picked it up.

'Lou! Tiff here. Come to Bet's quickly, please! She's in a bad way.' Tiffany sounded strange.

'What's wrong?' asked Louise, suddenly feeling faint.

'I think she will be OK. I found her in time. Just come now, OK?'

'Right, I'll be there.' Louise ran out the door and then ran back in again. 'Come on Sampson,' she said. 'We are going for a drive to Auntie Bet's.'

When they arrived at Bet's flat there was an ambulance parked outside with its lights flashing. Hugging Sampson to her Louise ran across the street and peered into the back. Bet was lying on the stretcher with an oxygen mask over her face. She was very pale and still. An ambulance officer was holding her wrist. Louise said to him, 'Oh God! Is she going to be alright?'

'Yeah. I think so. We'll get her to the hospital for oxygen therapy and she'll be OK then.' He paused, lifted Bet's right eyelid and peered into its glassy surface, nodding to himself.

'Appy Chrismit,' lisped Sampson to him. Louise had almost forgotten it was Christmas Eve.

'Happy Christmas to you too, young feller!' said the ambulance officer gruffly. 'We get a lot of these at this time of year.'

'What do you mean?' asked Louise, surprised.

'Lots of poor souls want to quit on life at Christmas time.

They don't want to have another Christmas alone. Without anyone they love. The TV makes it doubly difficult too. Rubs the whole family thing in. Really hard for them when they've got no one. This young lady was just lucky your friend Tiffany dropped by. Another hour — she'd have been a goner.' Louise gasped and tears sprang to her eyes. Tiffany came out of the house. Louise and Sampson hugged her and Tiffany burst into tears.

'Oh Louise!' she sobbed. 'I just can't believe it! That Bet would do this! She's so young, she's got us, our agency, money, this lovely house — everything to live for. Then she sat in the garage in her new car and started the engine. She sat there crying, holding a box of tissues and slowly getting carbon monoxide poisoning.' The two women stood rocking each other in the street with Sampson held between them in their arms. He was enjoying the hugging, lisping over and over, 'Appy Chrismit! Appy Chrismit!'

The officer climbed out of the ambulance. 'She's stable now. I'm taking her to the hospital.'

'I'm going to sit with her, wait till she wakes up, do you want to come?' asked Tiffany.

'No, I've gotta get to Mum and Dad's. They're expecting me. Let's have a cuppa first.'

They walked into Bet's flat. It was neat and elegant. Louise made coffee while Tiffany played with Sampson.

'How did you find her, Tiff?' asked Louise.

'I had asked Bet out for a drink tonight. I think she'd forgotten. So I came around to remind her and heard the motor running in the garage. I realised immediately what was going on. You sent me that e-mail ages ago, remember? You told me that Bet had said she had tried to commit suicide after Allen had left her the first time.'

'Has he left her now?' asked Louise, puzzled.

'I don't know. She had almost passed out when I found her. I opened the garage door and dragged her out as fast as I could. Urgh! What a horrible smell! Yuk. I couldn't do *that*. Not in a million years!' She paused and looked at Louise with love. 'I've got you, anyhow. Who would want to die with a beautiful woman like you in their life?'

Louise blushed. 'I'd begun to think you didn't want me any more, Tiff, that you just wanted to be friends. I want so much to be your lover and you won't let me near you. Is it because of Sam?'

Tiffany's eyes filled with tears. 'Yes. I'm finding it really hard to live without her, to get over our love, to be friends with her. It isn't fair to you to load you down with our relationship grief and old stuff. I'm sorry Lou, I really am sorry. I've made you promises and not followed through with them. I want to, soon. But it's Christmas now and everything's a bit chaotic.' Tiffany laid her head in Louise's lap and cried.

Louise stroked her hair and face. Her heart filled with love for Tiff, such a strong, loving, creative woman. A woman who was going to be her woman some day soon. She allowed herself to cry softly too, her tears falling into Tiffany's tangled auburn curls.

"on't cry, Mum,' begged Sampson. "on't cry.'

'It's OK, darling,' said Louise, hugging Sampson to her. 'Mummy's crying because she is very happy. It's Christmas Day tomorrow and we are going to Grandma and Grandad's tonight. Father Christmas comes tonight, remember?' Sampson brightened up immediately.

'*And* Mother Christmit?' he asked. Tiffany and Louise began to laugh hysterically.

'Mother Christmas *definitely* comes tonight,' said Tiffany holding Louise and Sampson tight.

19

In mid-January there was a meeting of all the partners at Tiffany's. Sam stood up first and paced around inside their conference circle of five sofas. She grinned with embarrassment and said, 'Well, I suppose I've gotta tell you sometime . . . I'm pregnant.' Everyone looked at Tiffany. She just stared at the floor and squeezed her fingers tightly together. When there was no explosion from Tiffany the rest of them relaxed and a babble of questions was fired at Sam.

How? Who is the father? Are you going to parent solo?

When are we going to meet your new girlfriend? Sam held up her hand.

'Stop, all of you. Daniella is the father of the baby. She is actually a male with a functioning dick and balls and she made me pregnant the first night we slept together.'

Shock was registered by everyone except Tiffany who continued to look glumly at the floor. She wiped her eyes with a tissue occasionally, Louise noticed. Sam was blushing and answering questions about the baby. 'He or she is due in August sometime. No, I don't know and I don't want to know what its sex is until it's born.'

'No, I'm not leaving Tiffany's just yet, if ever,' she stated, answering Fiona's question. 'I am a director just like all of you are and I want to stay with the Art Gallery contract as much as you want me to. I didn't do all that conceptual work and selling and ass-licking for nothing!'

Fiona leapt up from her seat, hugged Sam and said, 'Congratulations, Sam. I think it's wonderful that you have found a woman to make you pregnant. I can't wait to meet her, or him — whatever . . .' she laughed in happy confusion. 'Now I've got some news.' Everyone calmed down. Sam sat beside Tiffany and put her arm around her. Tiffany leaned on Sam and sighed. The relief was enormous.

Fiona looked around at them all and took a deep breath. 'My news is kinda the same. I'm pregnant to Jim and we are expecting the baby in October sometime.' Everyone clapped and whistled.

'I knew that would happen!' said Tiffany, laughing for the first time in ages. Then she blew her nose loudly.

'Wow!' said Louise, 'Sampson'll have serious company at the daycare centre!'

'Maybe we could get ourselves a group discount' suggested Sam jokingly.

'Jim has asked me to marry him,' continued Fiona. 'We have set the date for a month from now, the 20th of February. Of course all you darling friends are invited. Look at this gorgeous ring he's given me! He may look like my mother's idea of a hippie but he seems to have plenty of cash.' She flashed her left hand around. 'I plan on staying on at Tiffany's until I can work no more, like Sam. After the birth I will come back to work. Wouldn't it be great if we did all end up using the same daycare centre?'

'Make life easier,' said Louise.

'You lucky thing,' said Bet enviously. She sat in the corner of her sofa, pale but alive. Calm. Almost too calm, Tiffany thought, studying her.

'It looks like Tiffany's is going to be a family affair soon,' said Sam, laughter in her voice. She got up and hugged Fiona. 'Our kids will be like twins. Born a few weeks apart.'

'Yes,' said Fiona. 'Amazing, isn't it? We've both found the

man of our dreams!' They collapsed on their sofas laughing like crazy women.

'Bet?' asked Tiffany. Bet looked up from studying her hands and smiled wanly at Tiffany, raising her eyebrows. 'Anything to say?'

'Not really, no,' said Bet softly. 'Allen won't be home until next month. I'm just going to keep on working until then. I'm sorry about Christmas Eve. I won't do that again.' Louise moved over to Bet's side and hugged her.

'OK my friends,' said Tiffany in her organising voice. 'We have had a lot of ups and downs over the past few months and I reckon it is time for us to get together and have one of our parties. On Saturday night I want everyone to bring their partner of choice to the Istanbul. We'll need the big table this time.' She grinned, seeming happy for the first time since the night Sam had met Daniella.

'Good idea Sam?' Tiffany asked, raising her eyebrows at Sam.

'You won't get jealous if I bring Daniella along?' Sam was plumper, stockier now she was two months pregnant and had allowed her hair to grow longer. It remained zebra-striped. All her ear-studs had tiny silver Ds dangling from them.

Tiffany sighed. 'No Sam. I'm adjusting to the whole thing of you and Daniella – Danny. It will be a bit weird having a man who is more feminine than any of us but — if you are happy Sam, that's what counts. I promise I won't be rude to her — OK?'

Sam grinned. 'You better bloody not!' she growled and gave Tiffany a hug.

'Fiona?' asked Sam. 'You going to bring your real man?'

'Oh yes. If you girls want him along. I do hope he will cope with so much femininity around him!' Fiona was glowing. Beside her on the floor was a pile of wedding magazines.

'He's got more hair than all of us put together,' said Bet. 'Your kids probably won't suffer from baldness anyway.' She laughed. 'I'm not sure if I'll come on Saturday. I haven't got a partner to bring.' Her voice was ineffably sad.

'Aw — please come with us Bet,' urged Tiffany, Louise, Fiona and Sam.

'We never want to leave you out of anything,' said Louise. 'Come on, sweetie. Be ours for the night. We want you, no one else.'

'Well . . . Allen did mention he might be able to phone me later on . . . ' Bet looked at the floor.

'We can solve that problem easily,' said Louise briskly. 'Bring your cellphone to dinner and leave a message that you can be reached on it on his pager. That will do the trick, won't it? If he phones we will all be very noisy and give you no privacy, I promise.' She grinned and put her arm around Bet's shoulders and squeezed her tightly.

'OK, I will come then! Thanks, Lou. Who are you going to bring?'

Louise looked at Tiffany and said, 'Well, if I am very lucky, Tiffany may do me the honour of being my partner at our dinner. I've been waiting to be with her for a long time but it's only tonight that she has seemed to be ready for anyone new.'

Everyone looked at Tiffany. Sam grinned. 'I knew it all along,' she said smugly. 'I think that's why I left you. You were thinking about Louise and not about me. I can't stand that.'

Tiffany stiffened and then relaxed and grinned. 'Then you replaced me before I had really decided to replace you, Sam. You're a bloody fast mover.' She patted Sam on the shoulder and they leaned together like sisters. The others laughed. Tiffany slower than anyone?

Tiffany moved over to Louise and slipped her arm around her. Louise blushed and held Tiffany close. 'I *do* want to be with Lou,' said Tiffany. 'And I have put off starting our relationship because I was splitting up with Sam and didn't feel ready to become involved with Louise. It hasn't been fair to her but it's the best I could do.' She stood back from Louise and looked her in the eyes, taking hold of her hands.

'Louise. Tonight is the night for us. Are you willing?'

'Yes Tiffany, more than willing,' said Louise tears in her eyes, a brilliant smile lighting up her face.

'Come on then!' said Tiffany 'Let's go! We've waited long enough and Madeleine has everything prepared for us.'

Everyone at Tiffany's watched them leave.

'What did she mean?' Bet asked. 'Who is Madeleine?'

'Don't ask,' said Sam gruffly, getting on with her work.

20

$\mathcal{I}$ am trembling with excitement. It has been so hard waiting for Tiffany. When I am as horny for her as I am. As impatient as I am. I have had to subjugate myself, wait for her, as every good slave will wait for her mistress. Tonight will be the first time we really, truly make love. I sigh and tremble with desire and chills of excitement flood through me.

♋

I lead Louise blindfolded into the room Madeleine has allocated us. It is as luxurious as Madeleine's own room. I am glad I can afford the expense. Just to touch Louise intoxicates me. Her skin, the temperature of her body, her perfume, the long black silky fall of her hair, the fact that she is helplessly handcuffed and blindfolded. Mmmmm, it all arouses me so much I want to take her now!

But I won't. Oh no. We have waited so long for this night and it will be perfect. Perfection means relaxation, breathing deeply, thought, love, empathy and sustained cruelty to evoke the utmost ecstasy. Madeleine has taught me this over the last few months and tonight I will teach Louise.

♋

Tiffany unlocks the handcuffs and slips off the black silk scarf which covers my face. The room isn't much brighter without it but I can still see her. Standing feet apart, hands on hips, her legs gleaming black and a big white shirt covering her breasts. I don't get much time to look because she immediately orders me to strip off my clothes and kneel in the centre of the carpet.

All around me it is dark . . . there seems to be a bed somewhere, over there . . . I am afraid, I am alone. All I can depend upon is Tiffany. I obediently strip off my T-shirt, my jeans, my panties and crop top. It seems cold. My nipples contract and jut out.

I kneel on the carpet. I look down at the carpet. It seems right to look down. I must listen, really listen to her. My mistress will tell me what to do. I know she will.

I look long and lustfully at her. Louise trembles as she kneels naked in the centre of the dark red carpet. Beyond her the four-poster bed looms like a gallows or the promise of heaven. Around me are all the pieces of equipment I could ever dream of. God I hope I can remember how to get that damn strap-on dick settled just right. She deserves a good fucking . . . she needs a good fucking and so do I. Sweet beloved Louise.

'Crawl to my feet, slut!' I shout at her. She crawls toward me and I see the heart shape of her lovely ass preceded by her hair, an almost invisible glinting cascade, come to rest in front of me.

'Kiss my boots!' I demand and she does so, clumsily at first and then getting into it. Good girl, I breathe to myself. As a reward to this good slave girl I take the light whip of many fine strands of leather from my boot and begin to stroke her back and ass with it. Striking heavier and heavier by slow increments until I see light red marks all over her skin.

'Very good, little girl.' She has learnt that lesson of obedience easily.

♋

My body is tingling warm all over. Oh, my Tiffany, you were so gentle, so kind with your whip, you just stroked me! It felt so much sexier than a man's hands. Already my pussy is wet and you haven't even looked at me to check! I want you to look at me!

You don't. You order me to get onto the bed and lie on my back. I lie with my legs together but you pull them wide apart and tie them to the foot of the bed. I lift my head and I can't see what you have done to fasten my legs so firmly and so quickly. My legs are somewhere, they are not mine but yours now . . . it is magic.

You clasp something chill around my left wrist and pull my arm up and back, stretching my shoulder and then somewhere above me in the darkness chains chink and my arm is held over my head. I try to keep my right arm from being found by you but you are inexorable and drag it out from underneath me and pull it out to the same spread as the other.

You kneel over me. 'Naughty girl!' you say sternly and

twist my nipples until I squeal. Your gentle reproof. You move away, leaving me alone. All is silent.

I am firmly held and I test it. Arching back and forward I twist and turn against the firm bonds you have clasped tight to my naked wrists and ankles. I am vulnerable now, exposed to whatever you will do to me. There is no escape, none. My body heaves, panting, I feel a chill of real fear flow through me. I want to pee. Where have you gone? Tiffaneeee . . .

♋

I get the rest of the things I put aside for tonight and watch Louise for maybe half an hour as she struggles to get away from me. I can see her white skin glimmering in the dim light, the dark triangle of her pussy, the soft mounds of her breasts. I am deeply excited. My body grows strong and full of power as I think on how to feed her hunger and satisfy my own.

I will use the pounding, relentless, rhythm of her heart as my drumbeat. We will ride the rivers within us that alternately rage and softly flow. There will be heat that cools just enough to make time for long, slow, drinking kisses, but which sears again and demands a hard and stormy response.

Yes, sweet Louise, all this, all this for us! I breathe deeply

217

and calm myself . . . watching, watching, always looking at her.

♋

Suddenly I freeze in my struggles to get out of these bonds, my struggle to be calm, not to panic, not to pee myself. I see you standing there watching me struggle. Vainly I try to get away from your keen and haughty stare. I cannot. A bright light dazzles me. I can't see anything and the beam moves from my face to my breasts and then down to my cunt. It dazzles there a long long time. I blush as I think of you staring along that bright beam at my lewdly exposed pussy. I shaved it this morning, as you instructed me, I *hated* doing that. And now my wet pink nether lips ooze juices as you stare at them. I feel more exposed than if you had touched me.

You light a candle beside the bed and suddenly I see you. Your face is hard, serious, your white teeth seem sharper than usual, pointed perhaps.

A collection of straps and ties, metal and leather, is in your hands. Chinking, clinking, squeaking. You slip it over and under my tingling body, clinching the buckles tightly, slipping chill chains between my soft, slick pussy lips. Squeezing my breasts into firm leather cups that squash them flat.

I squeal as you tug my nipples through holes in the front of those tight cups. You are intent on your work. I love the firm feel of your hands, your focus on our desire. Each buckle has significance.

'This to keep your hot cunt faithful to me alone,' you say. 'This buckle to spare you another whipping, this buckle for your *first* orgasm and this for mine. These tit cups to remind your breasts and nipples that they are *mine* too.'

I lie there, ministered to by you; my chest heaves as I pant, awaiting your next desire. I have never been so deeply helpless or humiliated and a part of me wishes you could not see me like this, not know my needs. I am embarrassed by my desire to be a slave to another woman. Distantly I hear my mother shouting at me, shutting me in my room alone, the click of the key in the lock . . .

The shy girl part of me wants that we could be normal, whatever that is, be ordinary girlfriends and not mistress and slave, lover and lover. And another part of me wants this, whatever happens tonight, so much I know if you quit now I would just want to die.

Never leave this place. Just die now at your hands and feel the ecstasy of oblivion.

I buckle her into the best harness, it is one of Madeleine's favourites for naughty girls. As soon as I saw it I wanted it for

Louise and, by special arrangement, it is ours. It ties all around her body, giving her a feeling of constriction but laying all her sexual delights bare for my delectation. In addition I want her knees kept wide and her neck constrained with a high collar. I may want to lead her out to the viewing room to show her to Madeleine.

♋

You stand back and look at me again, my legs spread by a pole locked between my knees. My naked body cut into by tight black leather straps and chrome chains. Shiny buckles reflecting the candlelight. My nipples glowing as they peep out of the cups you forced over them. My neck encased in a tight dogcollar which means I cannot look anywhere but at you. I can see only you. Hear only you.

♋

I look at her for a long, long time. I pour a whisky and slowly, lingeringly drink it. In silence I watch Louise. I make her wait for her pleasure. Wait in darkness learning to trust me, trust how I love her, trust her own need to be restrained and experiencing small increments of discomfort and pain. I brush her cunt with my fingertips. I stroke the honey of her

220

inner body onto her nipples; she moans softly.

I walk away into the darkness and pick up two silver nipple clips.

☾

Time has no meaning. Your will, your wish is all that has meaning to me. You move away, I cannot see or hear you, I am afraid. Then a touch on the chains that bind my pussy and I am alight! Touches of wetness on my hot nipples then nothing. I lie, my senses seeking something, anything, my urge to pee stronger, ever stronger. Suddenly a searing pain fills my left breast, a cry leaves my throat. Then another sharp pain in my right nipple and my cunt is throbbing, full and open and my body arched with the shock of a pain which is replaced by a dull, cool ache.

☾

I pick up the vibrating wand, a converted electric toothbrush I found among Madeleine's collection. I begin to stroke it up and down the chains which cut tightly into Louise's sweet cunt. She gasps and wriggles. Held wide open she has no choice but to let me touch her most intimate parts with my magic wand. I watch as a pink glow suffuses her body then I transfer the vibration from her cunt to her lips. I press the wand between her lips and let her taste the exuberance of her own lust.

♋

I am on the violet edge of coming and you stop!

You move around the bed and undo the bonds that fasten me to it. You get onto the bed and snuggle into my back, stroking your warm hands and long beautiful nails up and down my back and sides, exploring my armpits, rummaging my breasts, smelling my hair. I sob softly in fear, in pleasure as your hands play me like a soft toy, moulded to your whims. Everywhere your hands go you pull and tweak the chains and straps and each tug sensitises my body more and more until each touch is an ecstasy I can barely stand.

I breathe deep and trust you deeper. This is such an essential need in me, to be controlled and wanted the way you want me. Just the way that you accept me and my needs and I accept and trust that you can fulfil them.

You kneel over me, pressing my head down into the bed. You pull your shirt aside, releasing your beautiful breasts. You rub them over my nipples, over my face, over my straps and buckles. You press your mouth to mine. I open, accept you, receive your tongue and lips with grateful joy. Our bodies flowing together in bliss, you lie on me and crush me to the bed. I surrender my breath to you, my heart beats even faster. I breathe only your breath and the taste of you is sweet.

Suddenly you rise off the bed and unbuckle my knees. As I slowly close my legs the pressure on my cunt from the chains is increased. I almost faint on the edge of coming. You press on my bladder and I realise you know I want to pee. You say nothing – but I am desperate!

'Undress me!' I order. With difficulty Louise gets up off the bed, her body stiff from the two hours she has been tied there. She is so tightly held in the harness that sometimes she has to struggle for breath.

'Yes my mistress,' she says, looking obediently at my booted feet.

'Follow me – on your knees!' I order her. I march over to sit on the throne. Immediately a spotlight comes on, focused on her, blinding her as she crawls, showing me my humiliated slave. She is at my feet, kneeling to begin unbuckling my high-heel boots.

There are many laces, many buckles and the sole and sharp steel-tipped stiletto heel press deeply into my naked thighs, almost cutting my skin, not quite. I enjoy the pain, the complex and dangerous task at hand. It takes my mind off my bladder. As each boot comes off I press your foot to my face and reverently kiss it. They are as beautiful as your hands.

I carefully place the boots aside and kneel, looking up at your face. Your feet rest in my lap, pressing over my pussy, kneading my belly, pressing on my full bladder, avoiding my clit. I am open under those chains, open and wet, my vagina begs for release, throbs and contracts and drips and drips again onto the chains, onto the floor. I MUST piss . . . oh goddess . . . I must!

You ignore my needs.

You slap my face for dallying, for kissing your feet when not ordered to do so.

I must not do what I am not told to do.

Tiffany orders me to take off her shirt. Under the shirt she has on a leather corselet. She stands and orders me to unlace it. Crawling carefully behind her, careful not to jog her in any way, I pull the laces out and under, through and down. The corselet goes over her head revealing her lovely breasts in all their fullness. Now she orders me to remove her leather pants. I slide up between her long beautiful legs, slipping my hands over her body, caressing her with my lips, biting gently, then firmly with my teeth. Her breath hisses in and I glance up. Her eyes are closed measuring the pleasure of me, my disobedience, against her plans.

My mouth settles on a nipple and I become mouse-like and then a mousetrap for each. She buries her hands in my hair, pulling it tight and tighter still. Trembling I unzip her fly. Her hands hold my teasing nipping mouth to her nipples in turn, her sighs and groans show me her pleasure and pain shared as my mouth pleasures her. I risk punishment but I do not care. I am hers and I worship her body. I am hers unto death.

I draw off the soft leather pants, slick against her real skin. The crotch is wet — soggy with her lust juices. Worshipping her I lay my body against her legs luxuriating in their strength.

Ahhhh — yes! At last Louise has me naked. As I have fantasised for so long! Over all the months of longing, desire, need, learning and planning that have brought us here to this night. She curves her hands over me, through me and at last, within me. Long fingers enter my cunt. I gasp and groan and then pull myself together. She is the slave and I, the mistress, will be strong and withhold my orgasm. She shall not have me so easily!

⊙

Tiffany! You are naked and I want to worship you. Crouching on the floor I beseech you to allow me to kiss you all over. I am full of lust and presumption. You kick me with your foot, disdaining me. You are a good liar. I see the juices of your lust dripping down your thighs. I know you are close to coming and I want to be responsible for that delight. You may come when you like. I must not. Not until I have permission. I do not have permission and I may not ask for it. You order me to kneel and I do so, legs wide apart, eyes down. I kneel on the soft red carpet and wait.

⊙

The time has come, I get the strap-on phallus, that most ancient of women's toys. I stand over Louise and make sure she watches as I slide one portion of the double-ended phallus inside my vagina. She sighs as it enters me. I shudder with the delight of that fullness enfolded by my hungry pulsating sex. I breathe deeply as I fumblingly fasten the unfamiliar buckles of the wide straps which hold it firmly around my hips. In front of me now thrusts out a very masculine-seeming cock. Better still, it is anchored inside me and each time I thrust into Louise, it will also thrust into me.

'Beg for it!' I order Louise as she kneels before me.

⊙

'Please, sweet kind mistress I beg you, fuck me with your gorgeous hard cock. The cock you wear only because of me, because of my greediness. Please mistress, oh please mistress I beg you, make my body yours and yours alone.' As I beg Tiffany looks haughtily down at me, grinning cruelly. Her eyes hot and wicked, full of plans.

She bends forward over the bed. 'Lick my asshole, slave!' she orders.

I crawl eagerly to her and begin hungrily to lick and suck. I can smell and taste her cunt as well as the sourness of her pink and brown hole. Again I almost orgasm but hold back, swaying on the cliff-edge of control. Full of vertigo I thrust my tongue into Tiffany, out around the phallus. Wickedly tasting her sweet cunt as much as I may. I pull her cheeks apart and suck and lick loudly. She trembles and I know she is as close as I . . .

⊙

'Enough!' I order and she stops that gorgeous sucking of my body. I know she is revelling in her humiliation and I am close to coming. I enjoy the fact that she needs to pee and I will not allow her. It will make the pleasure keener for her when I fuck her.

I order her to lie on the bed on her back. Trembling, she lies down and I push her knees wide apart exposing her pussy to my hungry gaze.

∞

My pussy is locked up by two chains on either side of my clit. My body is swollen around them. I long for them to be removed, for release from my bonds, for your permission to come. Far too slowly you unclip the clit chains and they slide slick and hot away from my open cunt.

'Beg me to lick you! Beg me, slave!'

'Please sweet mistress, lick my cunt I beg you!' I babble this over and over until you grab my nipples and twist them cruelly with the nipple clips. Again I almost come but I use an enormous effort of will not to. To restrain my body. I cannot come without your permission. The pressure on my pussy is unbearable from my aroused vagina and my full bladder.

Tiffany leans down and pokes out her tongue. Gently, too gently, she runs her tongue up and down my inner lips and over my firm clit. I almost scream in frustration, I squirm and moan in an agony of sensations and impatience. She leans away from me and grabs something. Pulls my body to the edge of the bed and shoves a pillow under my hips. Now my body is grotesquely exposed to the new spotlight which has just come on.

♋

She is so beautiful, totally exposed like this. I could watch her wet cunt for hours. I will watch it for hours one day, some day, when I am not so horny as I am today. I squirt lube on my fingers and thrust two into her tight little anus. She screams in surprise and I feel the pulsing of her orgasm starting. I wait, my fingers still within her, until I judge that the urge has receded a little, then I thrust in and out slowly until her muscles loosen. I gently introduce a slim flexible dildo into her ass and she clamps down on it. I lean forward and kiss her deeply. I love her so very much, the trust that she has in me. A precious jewel.

♋

You tease my inner lips with your big fat phallus while you twist my exposed nipples back and forth. Suddenly you thrust your phallus into me and we scream *Nnnnnggaaaahhhhhhhh!* as one at last. The pressure in my anus and my vagina and bladder have me exploding over and over in minuscule pulsations.

Slowly, maddeningly you thrust into me. Each thrust into my vagina makes an equal thrust into yours. Your hungry mouth finds mine, you bite my lips, my tongue, my cheeks and ears. Your strong hands pull my hair, you arch my body like a bow with the force of your fucking and pulling.

Your smile is that of the Devil and the maw of the sea crashing in ecstasy against the willing rocks of my body and my mind. My voice cries out heedless of meaning. I am childslave to the joy of you. Webbed, wide in ecstasy, my fingers wave wide upon the ocean. Sometimes anchored to you. Gripping your hair, your skin, your strong arms above me. Your nipples sweet stops of pleasure for my fingers, my lips.

The Pacific Ocean of your lust drowns me and I begin to shatter, crystal against magma.

'Permission please?' I beg in a wild whisper. 'Permission to come! Please?' I beg.

Did you hear?

Did you?

Will you hear . . .?

'Permission to come please!' I shriek as you fuck me harder and balls of fire begin exploding inside me.

Bolts of lightning shoot from you to me.

'Permission to come! Given!' you shout and at last, you flick my clit with your forefinger and I come, shrieking with each contraction, peeing myself around your cock, soaking the bed. Clawing the bed, the bonds restraining my body, bloodying your shoulders as you thrust in and out of my ecstatic shuddering body.

You thrust again and again, building up another climax within me. You seem limned with fire, with clouds. We are underwater and you are Neptune impaling me on your trident. All around us sea anemones surrendering to your power. I am blown up, bombarded. Energised by waves of power building, building. A great wild sandstorm. Bright colours tracing the contours of our pleasure engulf me. Exploding blues, fascinating pinks, rippling orange red, drowning green.

I cannot scream or breathe as your mouth closes over mine and you lock your nose to mine. We breathe in unison as you thrust in and in and on and on and suddenly my hand is trapped under the harness and you crush your clit against my fingers and you shout.

'YES!' you shriek, 'Yes!' as you come also, falling onto me, crushing me in bliss, burying your phallus even deeper into me . . .

♋

We sob together . . . shudder and shiver . . . Tiffany bites my shoulder and ear . . . trembling I lie spent beneath her.

'I love you,' I whisper from the depths of my being . . . 'I love love love you . . .'

'Louise.' The deep huskiness of her voice is all the love I need to know.

♋

Is it the ticking of the clock that wakes us? Outside the traffic roars and snarls through the city streets. At last we get to avoid rush-hour in Wellington. Just as well I arranged for Sampson to have evening daycare.

We smile, lazily, contented, into each other's eyes. I trace the outline of your eyes, lips, cheekbones. I kiss where my fingers touched. Your hands hold me as if you were drowning. Sinuously our bodies twine together, two kiwifruit vines, maybe male, maybe female, only we know our differences. Only we know the secret fruit formed on our branches. The ultimate intimacy of growth between us, through us. Melding together our bodies, roots, leaves, hands, breath, breasts and flowers . . .

♋

Madeleine knocked and entered the room later. She brought us each a glass of champagne.

'Wonderful! So loving . . . so loving,' she says softly, smiling. I see her smiles like a soft cloth covering spun steel razored surfaces.

'Let's go Lou,' you say. Restored to yourself after a glass of the bubbly.

'Yes, let's go,' I agree. Stretching lingeringly, languorously, full of an amazing calm, of peace. The stress and physical clamour of the last few months is somehow miraculously gone. My slate is clean and my feet barely touch the ground.

21

Allen McDonald walked up the stairs and admired the sign over the door of the advertising agency. 'Tiffany & Co' it said. He took out a bunch of keys, unlocked and pushed open the door, held it open for Jane, his speechwriter. The office was empty. It felt like no one had been there for days. The flowers in the vases were dead, rotted. Allen glanced around the silent semicircle of computer-laden desks as he allowed the door to close behind Jane.

'Here's where the best, the most creative, the only all-women-owned advertising agency in Wellington was based,' he said wistfully, waving his arms to encompass the big room. 'God knows if Tiffany will have the energy to get it up and running again.'

'What do you mean?' asked Jane, sitting on the big sofa in front of the harbour view.

'I suppose you haven't kept up with the news while you were away over Christmas?' He went to sit beside Jane and she turned towards him.

'Last Saturday night the Istanbul restaurant in Cuba Mall burned down and all the women who own Tiffany's were inside partying. It was their favourite place. Has been for years,' he sighed.

'Shit!' exclaimed Jane. 'I suppose the restaurant was full on a Saturday night? Did anyone get out alive? It's a very old building and it must have been cramped inside.'

'Yeah, amazingly. Almost everybody got out with just a few burns from falling drapery and smoke inhalation. I think they're all out of hospital now.' He sighed again. 'They reckon the fire was arson – but they say that about every fire in Wellington these days.

'Tiffany and Louise, Sam and her girlfriend Daniella got out really fast. They were nearest the door. Fiona pulled her fiancé Jim out and stuck his head under the bucket fountain in Cuba Mall. His hair and beard had caught fire. In fact there was only one fatality,' Allen continued sadly. 'My friend Bet.

You met her once. She was a partner here, at Tiffany's. She gave me the key I used to get in. She wanted to meet me here.'

'How come she died?' asked Jane clasping Allen's hand sympathetically in hers.

'She didn't move from her seat at the big table where they were dining. It would have taken only a few minutes for her to die, they say. The roof fell in pretty quickly and when they finally put the fire out and cleaned up the mess her body was found there. Where everyone had last seen her. She was still holding a wineglass in her hand.' He choked, sobbed, recovered himself. 'I think she wanted to die.'

'Didn't they realise she was in there and try to get her out?' asked Jane, horrified. 'Surely the fire brigade . . .?'

'Tiffany jumped into the fountain and wet herself all over and was about to run into the fire to get Bet when her friends stopped her. It was an inferno within a couple of minutes. There was nothing anyone could do. The place was full of cooking oil and fabric and candles. It was a dry old Victorian building and it just went – poof! Up in smoke.

'Tiffany is still hoarse from shouting to Bet over the roar of the fire. I saw her yesterday. She's devastated. She said, "I called and called her and she wouldn't move. I found her when she tried suicide on Christmas Eve. She had only just recovered. Personally I believe Bet wanted to die."'

Allen didn't tell Jane that Bet had loved him or that Tiffany had said Bet just couldn't handle being alone any more. That she couldn't stand living without Allen McDonald, MP for Southland. He began to sob. Jane put her arms around him and held him tight.

'I don't resent you, or anything like that,' Tiffany had said to him. 'I just wish Bet had been a stronger person, that's all. I know how much you meant to her. We all knew that. You were out of reach and there was nothing we could do to help her.' Then what hurt most. 'Maybe only *you* could have helped her, Allen.' He felt so helpless. No one had told him about the times Bet had tried suicide. She had never mentioned it. She had assured him she could handle being an MP's mistress. What could he have done from his country home in Invercargill?

Allen's tears eventually abated. His helplessness laid aside he sat up and used Jane's tissues to blow his nose and wipe his face. 'Thank you,' he said at last. 'You are as loving as my mother was.'

Jane raised her eyebrows at him and laughed. 'Is that a complement or an insult?' she asked. 'I'm not that old!'

He laughed too and sniffed. 'Oh, a compliment, definitely.' He smiled at her and stood up. He felt so much better now he'd had a good cry.

He wandered around the silent circle of five desks and

looked at the photographs of Tiffany's advertising campaigns that hung on the walls. He turned to his speechwriter and asked casually, 'Do you like the smell of baby powder?'